Kathleen The CELTIC KNOT

ceol

GIRLS *of* MANY LANDS

England ➳ 1592

Isabel: Taking Wing by Annie Dalton

France ➳ 1711

Cécile: Gates of Gold by Mary Casanova

Turkey ➳ 1720

Leyla: The Black Tulip by Alev Lytle Croutier

Ethiopia ➳ 1846

Saba: Under the Hyena's Foot by Jane Kurtz

China ➳ 1857

Spring Pearl: The Last Flower by Laurence Yep

Yup'ik Alaska ➳ 1890

Minuk: Ashes in the Pathway by Kirkpatrick Hill

Ireland ➳ 1937

Kathleen: The Celtic Knot by Siobhán Parkinson

India ➳ 1939

Neela: Victory Song by Chitra Banerjee Divakaruni

Kathleen: The CELTIC KNOT

by Siobhán Parkinson

Published by Pleasant Company Publications

For information, address: Book Editor, Pleasant Company Publications, 8400 Fairway Place, P.O. Box 620998, Middleton, Wisconsin 53562.

Visit our Web site at **americangirl.com**

Printed in China.
03 04 05 06 07 08 09 C&C 10 9 8 7 6 5 4 3 2 1

PERMISSIONS & PICTURE CREDITS

The following individuals and organizations have generously given permission to reprint illustrations contained in "Then and Now": p. 153—Tony Linck/TimePix (Dublin); pp. 154–155—Getty Images (dancing at the crossroads, refugee family); pp. 156–157—© Bettmann/Corbis (Dev); Brigid Kelly, from *Irish Dancing Costume* by Martha Robb, TownHouse, Dublin (1930s dancer); Getty Images (tenement); pp. 158–159—© Dallas and John Heaton/Corbis (modern costumes); AP Photo (Lord of the Dance); © Stephanie Maze/Corbis (Irish schoolgirls today).

Illustration by Troy Howell
Title Calligraphy by Linda P. Hancock
Photograph of Ms. Parkinson by Denis Mortell

Library of Congress Cataloging-in-Publication Data

Parkinson, Siobhán.
Kathleen : the Celtic knot / by Siobhán Parkinson ; illustration by Troy Howell.
p. cm — (Girls of many lands)
"American Girl."

Summary: Twelve-year-old Dubliner Kathleen Murphy is given the chance to take Irish dancing lessons in 1937 and discovers she has a talent for it.
ISBN 1-58485-748-X (pbk.) — ISBN 1-58485-830-3
[1. Folk dancing, Irish—Fiction. 2. Dance—Fiction. 3. Poverty—Fiction.
4. Dublin (Ireland)—History—20th century—Fiction.
5. Ireland—History—1922—Fiction.]
I. Howell, Troy, ill. II. Title. III. Series.
PZ7.P23935 Kat 2003 [Fic]—dc21 2002155611

To the 1930s generation
To my father and in memory of my mother
To all my uncles and aunts

Acknowledgments:
Thanks to Fr. Benedict Cullen, of the Capuchin Order, and to Peter Pearson, artist and architectural historian, for help with locating visuals on the Father Mathew Hall. Thanks also to my dad, Harry Parkinson, whose first-hand experience of life as a child in Ireland in the 1930s was invaluable.

Contents

1 *Late!* 1
2 *Mother Rosario* 22
3 *Brown Bread* 33
4 *Polly* 46
5 *Flying* 56
6 *The Letter* 67
7 *A Plan* 74
8 *The Conversion of Russia* 79
9 *Miracles* 86
10 *Bad News* 91
11 *Scarlett O'Hara* 102
12 *Cottage Industry* 112
13 *Celtic Knots* 116
14 *Curtains* 123
15 *The Cake from Jacob's* 139
Then and Now 153
Glossary 160

1 *Late!*

"Wake up, Kathleen!"

It was the sea that spoke, or that's what it seemed like, anyway, as the words lapped at my ear and then receded with a soft hiss, away from the shores of my consciousness.

"Kathleen!" came the hiss again. "Kathleen, wake up, like a good girl."

I turned my ear away, into the hard bolster. I didn't want to wake up. I wanted to sail off again to sleep, away to a dream country.

"Kathleen!" hissed the sea again, this time in my other ear, and the boat began to rock, it seemed.

Was there no getting away from it? Irritated, I opened my eyes.

It wasn't the sea and I wasn't on a boat. I was in my

own bed that I shared with Madge and Patsy and Lily, and Mam was shaking my shoulder and hissing at me to wake. As soon as my eyes fluttered open, Mam clapped her hand swiftly over my mouth and hissed again, "Not a word. Shush, don't waken the others."

"Why?" I asked sleepily, but my voice was muffled by my mother's cool hand over my mouth. The smell of Sunlight soap filled my nostrils.

"*Shh*."

It was dark, too dark for getting up.

"*Ay oh ah oo eh uh*," I mumbled. That meant, "I don't want to get up," but I could only manage vowel sounds with my mother's hand firmly across my lips.

"Shh," said my mother again. "I'm going to take my hand away now, but just whisper, all right?"

"I don't want to get up," I said again, softly.

"You don't have to. I just want to tell you."

What does she want to tell me? I waited.

"It's not getting-up time," my mother said. "It's only four o'clock in the morning. But I have to go out. Young Jimmy O'Brien came for me. His mammy sent him. Liz is in a bad way, and she needs me."

Liz was Jimmy's older sister.

"Liz O'Brien? Is she sick, or what?"

"No," said my mother. "It's her time."

My mother was a midwife. Not an official one, but she had attended more births than anyone in the Liberties—that was our area of Dublin, near the center—and she was always sent for when a woman needed help in the night. In the daytime, they could send for the Jubilee nurse, but at night people called on Mam, their neighbor and friend.

"Oh," I said, surprised. Liz was a young girl, not one of the married women my mother usually attended. "But Mam . . ." I forgot about being quiet and spoke aloud. "But Mam, she isn't marr—"

"Hush, can't you? You don't have to tell the whole street."

"But Mam, she can't—"

"Kathleen, I have to go. Now, listen. I want you to get the children up and give them their breakfast and make sure they're all at school on time. You can sleep a few hours more, but you'll have to get up early, do you hear me?"

"Eddy . . ."

Eddy was the youngest, only a baby.

"Your da will mind Eddy. The porridge is made from last night—you only have to put it on the range to warm it up. I've stoked up the fire. All you have to do is pull out the damper, and the fire'll start up and get good and hot in a few minutes. Can you manage that?"

"Why can't Da—"

"Kathleen!" My mother glared at me. "I haven't time to be arguing. Don't cross me now at a time like this, and I off to help a poor unfortunate girl."

"Sorry," I muttered. "But Mam, how can—"

"Children should be seen and not heard," said my mother.

This was the sentence I hated most in the world. I liked to be heard. I had questions bubbling inside me all the time, and I wanted answers to them. Where did the stars go in the daytime? If a girl was a Miss until she was married and then she was a Mrs., and if a boy was a Master when he was young, like Master Brick the Builder's Son in "Happy Families," why did he suddenly turn into a Mr. without having to get married? Did nuns wear shoes? If not, why not? Or if so, how come they made absolutely no sound when walking? If Mr. de Valera was against the government in our Civil War and his side lost, how come he was in charge of the government now? If St. Patrick was a Catholic, which obviously he had to be, how come the Protestants called their cathedral after him? And most puzzling of all, if only married people had children, how could Liz O'Brien, who was most definitely not married, be having a baby?

When Mam didn't want to answer a question, she had all sorts of little tricks for wriggling out of it, and the one about children being seen and not heard was the one she used most often. I was never sure whether she didn't know the answers or she didn't want to tell. That was another puzzle. If you wanted to know something, why couldn't grown-ups just tell you, instead of fobbing you off and telling you to go and play?

I would have to ask Polly. Polly always had an answer for everything. To tell the truth, I think she made the answers up half the time, but that was better than not answering at all, like the other grown-ups.

"Now, Kathleen, I want you to tell yourself to wake up again at seven. Can you do that?"

"How?" I asked.

"Knock your head against the bedhead seven times and say three Hail Marys."

"Does that work?" It didn't sound like much of a plan to me. I wished I had an alarm clock.

"It'd better," said Mam, "or you'll be in trouble. Do you hear me now? Listen, I have to run. Say a prayer for poor Liz."

I was up at seven, but it wasn't the head-banging and the Hail Marys that did it. I hadn't been able to get back to sleep—how could I, with my mother's threat ringing in my ears? So I lay wide-eyed in the dark, not daring to turn in case I woke my younger sisters, and wished the hours away until I thought it must surely be seven. Then I swung carefully out of bed and went into the kitchen, where the clock ticked on the mantelpiece, but, wouldn't you know it, it was only ten past five. I shuffled back to bed and tried to sleep again, but now my feet were cold because I'd walked barefoot on the lino, and if there's one thing

I can't do, it's sleep when my feet are cold. I usually stuck them up Madge's nightie and she warmed them for me between her knees, but I didn't want to wake Madge, and sure as eggs are eggs, I'd wake her if I stuck two icy spaugs under the hem of her nightdress.

Next time I got up to look at the clock, it was a quarter past six, and this time, when I wriggled back under the covers, I felt my body suddenly grow heavy and my eyes begin to droop. But now it was too close to seven to let myself drift off, and so I spent the last three-quarters of an hour half-sitting up, with my head lodged uncomfortably between the cold bars of the old brass bedhead, trying to stay awake.

On my third trip to the kitchen it was a couple of minutes to seven. I hurried back to the bedroom and raised the blind. Sunlight flooded the room, and I woke the girls. They thrashed about sleepily among the sheets like beached seals and moaned that they didn't want to get up. The lazy lot!

"You can have half an hour," I said, and I hurried away to put on the porridge. We had to leave for school by half past eight.

I pulled out the damper, as Mam had said I should, and immediately I could hear the roar of wind through the range, and I knew there'd be heat in the fire in no time. The porridge was a horrible, cold, glutinous lump in the saucepan, not a bit like the lovely, creamy, steamy stuff my mother ladled into our bowls in the mornings. How was I supposed to transform it from this glue-like substance into food? Was there something you added to it, to make it different? I wondered, but Mam hadn't said anything about that, so I just stuck it on the rangetop and shuffled back to the bedroom to get dressed.

"Where's Mam?" asked Patsy crossly, sitting up in bed, her hair all mussed and sleep in her eyes. She and Lily slept at the foot of the bed, and Madge and I slept at the top. There was more room that way, though sometimes you got a foot in your belly if one of the other two had a bad dream.

"Out," I said.

"At this hour of the morning? Where did she go? Is it the First Friday?"

My mother sometimes slipped out in the morning

early if she was "doing the First Fridays." This means going to Mass on the first Friday of the month for nine months in a row. That put you in God's good books and you could ask for just about anything, as long as it wasn't bad for you. Mam usually asked for Da to get a job. It worked, too, but when he did get a job, it never seemed to last. The factory closed or there was a strike or he got sick or something else went wrong.

"It's Monday," said Madge, emerging gloomily from under the covers at the other end of the bed.

"I hate Mondays," grumbled Patsy. "What's that awful smell, Katsie?"

"Don't call me that," I said, but I twitched my nose. "Oh, no!" I wailed. "The porridge!"

I ran to the kitchen, half-dressed, but it was no good. The porridge was ruined, bubbling away fiercely on the hot rangetop, half of it stuck to the bottom of the pot. I tried to spoon the top, unburned part out, but black bits from the bottom got mixed through it. The whole place stank but I couldn't open the window, because the top pane was cracked and Da had warned us all not to open it in case it fell out, because then he'd have to pay out good money to get it replaced. As long as it was only cracked, it was fine, but if it fell out, we'd freeze to death from the cold or starve to death from having spent our food money on glass.

The stench in the kitchen was unbearable. I opened the door out onto the landing to let the smell escape out into the rest of the house. The neighbors wouldn't like it, but I had to do something.

Da appeared from the other room, the one he shared with Mam and Eddy. It wasn't really a separate room. It used to be just an area of the kitchen with a curtain across it at night, but Da had put up a sort of wooden screen, to make it more private.

"Sorry, Da," I said, "about the porridge, I mean."

"Kathleen Murphy, you are a disgrace. Will you go and cover yourself!"

I looked down at myself. I was in my slip. I could feel myself going scarlet. I raced into the bedroom and flung on the first clothes I could find, an old gray skirt and a blue cardigan.

When I came back into the kitchen, Da was trying to prise the window open, gently, so as not to disturb the damaged pane. It was twenty to eight by the kitchen clock.

"I'm sorry, Da," I said. "Wasting good porridge like that." I was ashamed of myself. I knew we could ill afford it.

"Ah, sure, it could happen to a bishop," said Da forgivingly.

"It couldn't," I said. "I bet a bishop wouldn't be cooking the porridge. I bet he'd have someone to do it for him. An altar boy, maybe."

"Get away out of that," said Da with a laugh.

"What'll we have for breakfast now, Da?" I asked. "Is there any more oatmeal?"

"There are, but if we eat tomorrow's porridge today, there'll be no porridge tomorrow, and then we'll have some explaining to do to your mother. No, I'm afraid you girls'll have to go to school with no breakfast, just the cuppa tea."

I could feel my stomach rumbling already. But that wasn't the worst part. The worst part was that my sisters would have my life for burning the porridge and making them all go to school hungry.

"Or maybe . . ." said Da, and he lifted the lid off the bread crock. "We're in luck, alannah. There's half a loaf. If you cut it very thin, there'll be enough for everyone. You slice it, and look sharp, as the fork said to the knife. I'll put on the kettle for the tea."

Bread was better than nothing. It filled you up, but it didn't warm you through the way porridge did.

Then I had a brain wave. "We could make fried bread, Da. That'd be something hot to eat."

"Sufferin' ducks!" said Da, letting on to be shocked. "What do you think it is, your birthday or what? And you after burnin' the porridge!"

"Ah, Da!" I said. "Go on!"

"You go and get the rest of them up and I'll put on the pan, so," said Da, with a sigh that was far too loud and dramatic to be real. "I think there's a bit of dripping there somewhere, if I can lay my hands on it."

"Thanks, Da," I said.

I checked the clock. Nearly eight.

Patsy and Madge were nearly fully dressed, but Lily couldn't do up the buttons properly on her cardigan, and she had her shoes on the wrong feet, too. I sorted her out, and then I had to make Madge undress again because she'd forgotten her bodice. Bodices were horrible old underthings, but Mam always said that children had to wear their bodices from September to June, or they would catch their death of Old Moany. That was her joke word for pneumonia. I didn't know what pneumonia was, exactly, except that you caught your death of it, and even if I had burned the porridge, I wasn't going to have my sister catching her death. "Catching your death" sounded much worse than just plain dying, like old people did, because it seemed to mean that it was your own fault and you had only yourself—or your careless elder sister—to blame.

Next came the hair brushing. This was bad, because all three of my sisters wailed and squirmed when it was being done, even though they had short hair, cut just below their ears and with fringes across their foreheads, because it was supposed to be easier to keep. I had long hair, which was murder to brush in the mornings, but that lot had only to catch sight of the hairbrush to start up whining and roaring.

Then came the ribbons—a blue one for Madge, a

green one for Patsy, and a yellow one for Lily, who had to have everything yellow, because it reminded her of sunshine. I wasn't much good at making bows, but I did my best. They didn't seem to notice that their hair ribbons were "a bit on the Kildare side," as Da said.

By the time all that was done, it was a quarter past eight, and Da had a small pile of fried bread on a plate in the middle of the kitchen table and mugs of steaming tea for everyone. He'd halved all the slices, to make the bread go farther.

Patsy got grease from the fried bread all down her blouse, so of course I had to hunt for a clean one for her. There wasn't a clean one, but I found one of my own that I thought would do her. It was a bit big on her, and Patsy said she wasn't going out in that, she'd look like a tinker. That made Da cross. He was from the country and he always had a kind word to say about the tinkers, who roamed the countryside and were available for odd jobs when the farmers were at their busiest. He said there was nothing wrong with the tinkers and not to be talking like that about people who were worse off than ourselves, God bless the mark. That made Patsy crankier than ever and she said she wasn't going to school looking like a person worse off than herself, then.

I had another search in the bedroom and found Patsy's other blouse, which looked the worse for wear, but at least it was better than the one with the streak of grease on it. Patsy muttered about it, but I gave it a quick sponge-down with a dishcloth, and in the end Patsy said she would wear it. That girl will be the death of me, always finding something to moan about.

Half past eight and the dishes not washed. I piled everything into the sink and looked at Da.

"It's all right," he said. "I'll do them."

"Thanks, Da," I said, and I filled the kettle again for him, so he'd have hot water.

Then I had to brush crumbs off Madge's cardigan and look for her raincoat for her, because she couldn't remember where she'd left it.

"Sure, I'm a star turn as a washer-upper," said Da, and he started to sing. "'Twinkle, twinkle, little star, How I wonder—' What do I wonder, Kathleen?"

"'What you are,'" I shouted from the bedroom,

where I was gathering books and schoolbags.

"'How I wonder what I am,'" sang Da. "That's not right," he muttered to himself. "That's not right, Kathleen. 'What I am' doesn't rhyme with 'little star.'"

Madge started to giggle. Patsy giggled, too.

I came out of the bedroom.

"Sing it for me so, if yous are so smart," said Da.

Eddy appeared out of the other bedroom. He stood in the doorway sucking his thumb, but as soon as Da said to sing, he took out his thumb and started up. "'Tinkle, tinkle, little tar.'" His nappy needed changing, I could see that, but I didn't say a word. I hoped Da would do it after we'd left.

"'How I wonder what I am!'" Lily joined in, grabbing Eddy by the hands and dancing around the kitchen with him.

"Where do the stars go in the daytime, Da?" I asked. I shouldn't have. I didn't have time, but it was one of the questions that had been bothering me for ages.

"I'll show you," Da said, and he reached into the press and brought out a stub of a candle. "Watch now," he said, and he lit the candle with a twist of paper from the range.

I watched.

"Well?" said Da. "What do you see?"

"I see a flame," I said.

"Yes, but is it a very bright flame? Is it as bright as it would be if the room were dark?"

"No," I said. "It's hardly there at all, Da."

"That's it. You see, a small light is hardly visible in the morning sunshine. Same with the stars. They're still there, only we can't see them in the daytime, because it's too bright."

He leaned over and blew out the candle.

"You should've been a teacher, Da!"

"Would you look at the time!" Da said. "Get out of my sight!"

I had the girls' schoolbags in my hands, all stuffed—I hoped—with the right books and copies.

"Come here to me till I put these on you," I said. "Come on, look sharp." I sounded just like my mother.

"As the fork said to the knife," said Da. Da sounded like himself, as usual.

Ten to nine and we clattered down the stairs and

out the door. We passed by the toilet just inside the street-door opening, pinching our noses with our fingers and thumbs. All the passing drunks used it during the night, and it stank permanently. Our family never used it. We had a chamber pot in the bedroom, but mostly we had trained ourselves to hold on till we got to school. My mother said we would get a disease if we used the house toilet. She said it was full of germs, which when I was younger I used to think was a slang word for "Germans." That was enough to put me off. I'd heard all about the Germans from my granda, who'd fought in the Great War. And now there was that Hitler fellow who was always yelling on the wireless; he didn't sound a bit nice. But even without the threat of Germans, I wouldn't have wanted to use the toilet anyway. The floor was always ankle-deep in water—or worse—and the smell was disgusting.

We flew through the streets, our schoolbags bouncing on our backs as we ran, dodging in and out between the old women with their shopping bags, waiting impatiently while the buses trundled by. We were nearly at the school and going like the clappers when Madge fell at the curb and cut her knee.

There was no time to go home to wash it, so I whisked out my hanky and spat on it. Madge said she didn't want my old spit on her sore knee, but I said spit was good for healing. I didn't know if that was true, but I had to say something. I couldn't let Madge go to school with dirt on her cut—she might get blood poisoning, which was worse than pneumonia, I knew that. It ran through you and killed you stone dead in a matter of hours. Madge screamed when I dabbed at the cut, but I held on to her leg for dear life and I kept going, finally managing to get the grit out of it. Then I kissed it, which made Madge scream even more, but my mam always kissed sore spots, and I thought it might help. I could hear the school bell clanging.

"Come on!" I called to the others. "We're late!"

The school bell gave a final clang as we got to the gate. A nun was just coming to lock it. The nuns always locked the gate at bang on nine, and if you weren't on the right side of it, you were in trouble. We raced across the road as the gate came swinging toward us. I made a dive forward, pushing the other three ahead of me and into the closing gap. They lurched and stumbled, but they made it to the other side. I didn't, though. The gate came clanging against the gatepost as I stepped forward, and the bar came down right in front of me with a clatter and settled into position. I put up my hand to open it, but the nun rattled the bars.

"No pushing," she shouted. "I'm locking it. It's after nine."

"It's not! It's not!" I squeaked desperately, shaking the gate.

A clock started up then, from the tower of the nearest church, ringing the hour, so I knew it couldn't have been nine o'clock when the nun closed the gate. I pointed in the direction of the ringing, but she shook her head. It was Sister Eucharia, the one who never smiled. Her face looked as if it were made out of bacon fat—it was dirty white and featureless. I stood there while the clock rang out the hour, still pointing hopelessly toward the church tower. Sister Eucharia pushed her fingers in at the side of the starched white bib she wore on her chest and pulled a large man's watch out of a pocket that was hidden behind it. She held the watch up, face out, between the bars of the gate. It showed a minute past nine. The church clock must have been slow—or else Sister Eucharia's watch was fast. The old rip, she could have given me the benefit of the doubt.

I slumped dejectedly against the locked gate, feeling the iron cold against my forehead. It was my third time to be late this term, and that meant I had used up all my chances—and now I would be in for it.

2 *Mother Rosario*

When all the girls had filed into the school, Sister Eucharia came back to the gate to let me in. She sent me straight to Mother Rosario's office.

"Well, madam?" said Mother Rosario icily, by way of greeting.

Everyone said the head nun was strict but fair, but I had never noticed the fair part. I knew she always called girls "madam" when she wanted to show her displeasure.

"What have you got to say for yourself?" Mother Rosario went on.

"Sorry, Mother," I said in a small voice. I tried to sound very humble and contrite. Nuns liked that.

"I don't mean that. I mean, have you got an excuse, girl? Speak up, now. If you have a good reason for

being late, maybe we could overlook it this once."

That must be the fair part, I thought, but it wasn't much good to me. I couldn't possibly tell Mother Rosario that my mother had gone out in the night to attend a birth. Nuns didn't understand these things. They had no children. They lived in a convent and said their prayers. Birth and babies, getting my sisters' hair brushed in the morning, helping my da make the breakfast, and what a disaster burning the porridge was—it was all too difficult to explain. If a nun burned the porridge, they probably just threw it out to the pigs and made more. Nuns wouldn't understand what it was like to have to count every slice of bread, every spoon of oatmeal, and I certainly wasn't going to tell Mother Rosario and bring shame on my family. Nuns were notorious snobs. Then there was the added complication about Liz O'Brien not being married. I knew for sure that I mustn't let that slip to the nuns, or I might bring even worse shame and retribution down on my family and neighbors. Unmarried girls weren't supposed to have babies—I knew that much.

"Madge fell and cut her knee, Mother," I offered helplessly. "I had to clean it for her."

"I see. She fell because you were late and running to school?"

"Yes, Mother."

"And why were you so late that you had to race over the roads, like corner boys, instead of walking at a brisk and steady pace, like young ladies?"

"Patsy got grease on her blouse, Mother." It wasn't working, I knew that, but I couldn't find a way to explain the piled-up details that had made the morning go all wrong.

"Indeed?" Mother Rosario's very black eyebrows disappeared under the stiff white forehead band that hid her hair and held her long black veil in place.

"Because we had fried bread for breakfast," I went on.

"Well, aren't you well off! Fried bread, indeed!"

I didn't know how to answer that one. It hadn't occurred to me that fried bread was some sort of awful luxury that I shouldn't dare to mention for fear of offending the nuns. It was never very clear to me what would offend the nuns. They seemed to think differently from ordinary people.

"Yes, Mother," I murmured hopelessly.

"Well?"

"Well what, Mother?"

"Don't give me cheek, Kathleen Murphy!"

"Sorry, Mother. I burned the porridge."

"You burned the porridge. Well, now we're getting places. Wasn't that careless of you?"

"Yes, Mother. And then I had to find a clean blouse for Patsy and Da was singing some stupid song and the girls were giggling and Eddy was singing too, and I was in a rush. I didn't sleep last night, I was up all night looking at the clock in the kitchen, and—"

"Enough!"

I stopped.

"Sorry, Mother," I murmured again, looking at the

floor, wishing it would open up and swallow me whole.

"It seems to me, Kathleen, that you are blaming everyone but yourself here. Madge fell. Patsy tore her blouse. Your father—"

"No, Mother, it was grease. Patsy got *grease* on her blouse."

"Kathleen!" Mother Rosario's voice was like thunder now. "Will you stop blathering and rawmayshing! Greasy, torn—it doesn't matter. The point is, you are deflecting all the blame for your tardiness on to your unfortunate family, aren't you?"

"No, Mother."

"Don't contradict me, child!"

"No, Mother. Sorry, Mother."

I could feel tears running down my face. I licked my lips. Salt.

"Sorry, Mother," I said again, in a tiny voice, willing the nun to stop torturing me, to just slap me and let me go to my classroom.

Mother Rosario stood up and came around to the front of her desk. She wore giant rosary beads suspended from her waist, like all the nuns. But in addition to this, because she was the head nun, she also carried a gigantic bunch of keys and a wide, flat *slat*, which she used to slap people on their upturned palms.

She was right, of course. It *was* my fault. If I hadn't asked Da the stupid question about the stars, we'd have made it.

I closed my eyes and screwed them up hard, held my breath, and held out my hand for a belt of the *slat*.

Nothing happened. I waited, hand outstretched, wishing the nun would whack me and get it over with. Three on each hand was usual. I hoped I wouldn't have to have more than that. Three was just about bearable. It hurt horribly at first, and it went on stinging for hours, but it didn't break the skin or cause bruising. You could even write within an hour or so, though your hands burned.

Still nothing happened.

I opened my eyes. Mother Rosario was looking at me.

"There's no need for that," Mother Rosario said in a voice that was almost kind. "But I'll have to see your mother, Kathleen. I can't have girls coming late to school with no reasonable excuse and looking like the wreck of the *Hesperus*."

I dropped my hand to my side. *The wreck of the Hesperus!* I looked down at myself for the second time that day. I was still wearing the old clothes I'd thrown on in a rush that morning. I'd forgotten to change into my neat school skirt and blouse. And now I remembered that with the fuss about brushing my sisters' hair, I had forgotten all about my own. I put a hand to my head and, sure enough, my hair was good and tangled—I could feel the knots under my fingers. I must look a right mess.

But that was a minor point. My mother was being sent for! That was the worst possible punishment, because it meant I'd be in trouble at home as well as at school, and then I'd have nowhere where I could feel safe and free.

"No, Mother, please don't. I'll be good. I won't be late again."

I could feel the tears coming again, and now there was a drip coming from my nose, too. The embarrassment of it! I wiped it quickly with the back of my hand and fished up my sleeve for my hanky, but of course it was streaked with dirt and blood, and I stuffed it quickly back up my sleeve again before Mother Rosario could see it.

"Kathleen, Kathleen, you don't understand."

Then the unbelievable happened. Mother Rosario dipped into the deep pocket of her long, long black nun's skirt and produced a huge, starchy clean, blue-and-white-checked handkerchief and handed it to me. I didn't know what to do with it. I couldn't possibly put it to my nose and soil the holy nun's hanky.

Mother Rosario took the hanky back and dabbed at my tear-streaked cheeks herself, and swiped at my nose and mouth with it, too. Then she handed the hanky to me again and said, "Keep it for today. You can wash it and bring it back to me another time."

I nodded disbelievingly, crumpling the handkerchief between my fingers. I would rub it and scrub it and rinse it and starch it and iron it until it was a perfectly crisp square again.

"Now, listen to me, my child," the nun went on. "I need to see your mother, just to make sure everything is all right at home. I find that when good girls start coming late and giving back answers—"

"I don't give back answers!" I wailed.

"There, you're doing it now!" said Mother Rosario. "I find that when girls who are usually good start misbehaving, it often means there is trouble at home, and I just want to satisfy myself that this is not so in your case."

"It's not, Mother, I swear. Cross my heart and hope to die. There's nothing wrong at home."

I couldn't bear the thought of Mam being humiliated by the nuns poking their noses in and asking personal questions about our family life. She would die of shame.

"We don't swear, Kathleen."

"No, Mother, but really, there's no need to send for—"

"Let me be the judge of that, Kathleen. Now, you go on to your class and tell Miss Glynn that you were with me and it's all right, you're not to be punished. Tell her I'll speak to her later. Have you got that, now?"

"Yes, Mother."

"And here, Kathleen." Mother Rosario opened a small stripy pink tin she had on her desk and extracted a bull's-eye. My eyes opened wide. "You'll want to suck that fast now, so it's gone by the time you reach the classroom."

"Thanks, Mother," I whispered and slipped the bull's-eye into my mouth. The sweet, pepperminty taste spread immediately, deliciously, over my tongue.

"And don't worry, I won't upset your mother. I just need to talk to her. Tell her to come in tomorrow. It'll be all right."

I pushed the sweet into the side of my cheek with my tongue and managed another "Thanks, Mother," as I turned to go.

"Mother?" I asked then, stopping.

"Yes?"

"Mother, was Saint Patrick a Catholic? Only how come the Protestant cathedral is called after him?"

Mother Rosario looked at me and shook her head. "That's too complicated for today," she said.

She was as bad as my mother, evading questions. At least she hadn't said, "It's a mystery," which is what nuns usually said when you asked them something about religion that they couldn't answer. I sighed, but I didn't argue. I just trotted off to my classroom, sucking the bull's-eye as hard as I could. I needed to get it down to a manageable size before I reached the door, so I could store it neatly inside my cheek and still be able to speak clearly to my teacher, Miss Glynn.

3 *Brown Bread*

Mam was furious at being summoned to the school. She didn't know who to be more annoyed with, me or Mother Rosario.

"I have a good mind to give you a walloping over this, Kathleen. Can I not trust you to behave yourself at school and not be drawing attention to yourself?"

"Sorry, Mam," I said. I seemed to be saying nothing but "sorry" these days.

"And as for that Rosario one, I'll give her a piece of my mind, you mark my words."

I was shocked to hear the head nun referred to by her name, without the respectful title "Mother."

"Mam, don't show me up in front of the nun!" I pleaded. "You know what nuns are like. If any of the mothers stand up to them, they take it out on us."

This didn't exactly fit with the kindness of Mother Rosario yesterday, lending me a hanky and giving me a sweet, but all the same, I didn't want to risk getting into deeper trouble. And it was true that the nuns didn't take kindly to mothers who "interfered."

"We're as good as they are any day," said my mother stoutly, though she knew that wasn't how the nuns viewed it. Everyone knew that if you came from the tenements, the nuns were much harder on you than if you came from the Artisan Dwellings, which were the neat, yellow-brick, two-up-two-down houses, where the better-off workers and tradesmen lived. The nuns thought they had a better chance of making something of those girls than of the daughters of the poorest classes—that was us—who would only marry young and produce broods of sickly, dirty children, many of whom would mercifully die young. The awful thing was, it was true. Our neighbors were always having babies, and half of them died before they were a year old. It was terrible.

"Tuppence looking down on three ha'pence," muttered Mam proudly, pulling on her best Sunday coat and ramming her smart black hat with the cocky little feather in it over her springy curls. It was the hat she wore "on only state occasions and bonfire nights," as she put it herself.

"Oh, Mam, don't be going on like that!"

"Like what?"

"Being all proud and everything. Nuns like you to be humble."

"We'll see about that," said Mam, and she picked up her handbag. She had nothing to keep in a handbag, but she carried it all the same when she was dressed up, for the look of it. It rode on her hip, held in place by the straps that she kept tucked into the crook of her elbow.

I trotted along beside her, wishing to goodness this day was over, and giving her instructions all the way about what she was to say and what she wasn't to say to Mother Rosario. My little sisters trotted along behind us, quiet for once and listening hard.

"Don't say you were at a birth, Mam," I begged.

"Don't tell me what to say, Kathleen," said Mam grimly. "It's time those nuns heard something about how real people live."

"Mam, you'll make a holy show of me!"

"I had to attend a neighbor in an emergency," Mam said to Mother Rosario when we were shown into her office. "In the middle of the night. That's why Kathleen was late for school."

I looked at my feet. I lined up my two brown toecaps and stood very still.

"An emergency, Mrs. Murphy?"

Please don't let her say it. I could feel a blush creeping up my cheeks. I kept my eyes fixed on my feet.

"Yes, Mother, a . . ." My mother searched for the formal word. "A confinement," she said.

"I understand," said Mother Rosario.

"Young Liz—"

I squeaked in terror. "Mam!"

"Well, it doesn't matter, the poor gir—the poor woman was in a bad way. Hemorrhaging to beat the band, Mother."

I blushed harder. Hemorrhaging—that was blood. Why did she have to mention blood?

"I'm sorry to hear it," said Mother Rosario.

"Anyway, I had to leave Kathleen in charge of the younger ones, and, well, a few things went wrong. She's only young, she hasn't much experience, you can't blame her for being late, Mother—"

"Mrs. Murphy, we are not here to blame Kathleen for anything. I just wanted to have a little chat with you, to make sure everything is all right at home. Your husband is out of work?"

This time it was my mother who blushed.

"The factory closed down, Mother. He had a good job, he was foreman, but . . ."

"Please, Mrs. Murphy, I don't wish to pry. I just wondered if he would be interested in a bit of work in the convent gardens? Just a few hours a week, but he could do it in his own time, when it suits him. Our gardener is getting on, coming close to retirement. He needs a hand, and if we find the right assistant, well, who knows, the job will come up in a year or two . . ."

Assistant gardener, and working for the nuns.

Da wouldn't think much of that, but at the same time, well, you know what they say—beggars can't be choosers. I held my breath.

"I will mention it to him, Mother," said Mam. I could hear that she was pleased. "Thank you," she added.

"Right, well now, with regard to young Kathleen here, can you assure me that everything is all right at home, nothing is worrying her?"

"She's fine, Mother. Nothing like that. She's a good girl, only that she asks so many questions."

"That reminds me," Mother Rosario said, turning to me, "about your theological question."

What was she on about?

"Saint Patrick lived at a time before Catholics and Protestants parted company. He was a Christian, and he belongs to all Christians. Does that answer your question?"

"Yes, Mother," I whispered, but I'd have to think about that one. We children always thought the devil lived in the Protestant church, but that couldn't be true if they were Christians, too.

"I believe she's talented," Mother Rosario went on, speaking to my mother again.

"I beg your pardon, you believe . . . ?"

This was clearly the first time my mother had heard it, and it was news to me too. I was terrible at school, always getting my sums wrong. I wasn't much at spelling either, though my handwriting was not too bad, and the teacher never asked me to read out my compositions, the way she did with the brainy girls. I always came last in the races on sports day, too. I didn't see where this talent of mine could lie.

"Musical, Mrs. Murphy. I hear she has a lovely voice."

Right enough, I was always humming and warbling about the place, though I'd never thought of it as being "musical." Everyone in my family sang. Irish songs, like "Molly Malone" and "Are You Right There, Michael?" Songs we learned off Polly's wireless, like "Stormy Weather" (that was Da's favorite). Hymns, sometimes, too, like "I'll Sing a Hymn to Mary" and "Sweet Heart of Jesus." (Patsy brought the house down one day when we sang that. She said she didn't know

Jesus had a sweetheart. Mam made her wash her mouth out with soap, the poor little girl. But she wasn't trying to be funny or disrespectful—she just misunderstood.)

"Musical?" said Mam, wonderingly. She'd obviously never thought of it that way either.

"Now, I know you probably . . . if you'll forgive my saying it, because I don't wish to be indelicate, but you probably can't aff—I mean, you probably haven't got a piano at home?"

"No, Mother."

I winced at my mother's tone. You could cut it with a knife, as Da would say.

"She could practice on one of the school pianos, of course, if she wanted to take lessons. It would help her develop her talent and encourage some discipline."

"Piano lessons? Mother Rosario, I think . . ."

"Well, maybe not, Mrs. Murphy. Perhaps you're right. But what would you think about dancing lessons? That might suit a musical child."

"Dancing? What sort of dancing, Mother? Tap dancing? Ballroom dancing?"

"Irish dancing, Mrs. Murphy. Part of Our National Heritage. Lots of our girls do it. It's a lovely accomplishment for an Irish girl. And it gives them an interest, keeps them out of harm's way, you might say."

My mother wasn't very keen on "Our National Heritage." Her family had all been on the Treaty side in the Civil War. The pro-Treaty people, like Mam's family, had wanted to settle with Britain after the War of Independence and get on with building up the new state; but the anti-Treaty people, led by Mr. de Valera, thought that the agreement with Britain wasn't favorable enough to Ireland and wanted to keep on fighting for a better deal. The Civil War had happened before I was born, of course, when my parents were young. But even though it was all well in the past by now, my mother still didn't trust Mr. de Valera, who *was* very big on Our National Heritage. Mam half-believed that Irish dancing, Gaelic football, and the Irish language had been invented more or less single-handedly by Dev—as everyone called Mr. de Valera—to make out that we were more Irish than we really were. She was wrong about that, of course, but that was the way her mind worked, and it wasn't easy to change her opinions.

Da was a Dev man, and he was delighted with the new constitution Dev was after bringing in, but Da kept his views to himself when Mam got up on her hobbyhorse and started in on politics. Dev was very keen on happy maidens dancing at the crossroads, but it was a long way from the crossroads to the tenements of the Liberties, Mam always said, and Our National Heritage didn't put bread on the table and that was for sure.

I hoped to goodness she wasn't going to give this little pet lecture of hers to the nun. The last thing I wanted was for the two of them to get stuck in a political argument, but I knew perfectly well that, for two pins, Mam would do it.

Luckily, she toned it down a bit. "We aren't very Irishy-Irishy in our house, Mother," she said at last. "My father survived the Great War but was nearly murdered by his own countrymen when he got home. I don't think much of that kind of Irishness, and I don't approve of this Economic War business, either.

I say, let Ireland and England live like neighbors and get on together and forget the past. We all need each other in this world, is how I view it, and if you ask me, Ireland's refusing to trade with England is cutting off our nose to spite our face. Sure, you only have to look at the state of the country, with half the men out of work and the farmers in a terrible state."

Mother Rosario laughed. That made me jump—I'd never heard that before.

"My goodness, you are very well-informed about politics, Mrs. Murphy," she said. I knew Mam wouldn't like that. Why wouldn't she be well-informed? Being poor didn't mean you had to be ignorant. "And you are not entirely wrong, I dare say," Mother Rosario went on. "But I'm sure you have no actual objections to Irish dancing?"

"Well, no, I suppose not, Mother. I suppose it's harmless enough."

"Certainly it is harmless, Mrs. Murphy, and better than harmless. It is wholesome and healthy, too. Great exercise, you know, as well as being patriotic."

Sounds like brown bread, I thought. *Good for your*

bowels as well, in all probability. But I said nothing. I didn't dare.

"As I say, it keeps a girl occupied in a ladylike sort of way. It's not like other, pagan forms of dancing—and very few boys, Mrs. Murphy, though I dare say Kathleen isn't thinking along those lines just yet."

I blushed again, but luckily nobody was looking at me.

"All right, so, Mother," said Mam meekly. "Since you seem to think so highly of it, sure, maybe we could give it a try."

"Well said, Mrs. Murphy. I am sure Kathleen will love it. Some of the other girls in her class do it. Let me see—Annie Ruane, and Brigid Mullane, and Tess O'Hara—they love it, they just love it."

I winced again. Tess and Brigid and Annie were the snootiest girls in the class. I wasn't going to like being lumped in with that lot of stuck-up misses. My own friends, Angela Doyle and Nell Carty, would desert me for sure if I took up with that shower. Besides, they had all been dancing since they were six years old and were sure to be miles better at it than I would ever be.

I wished I could catch Mam's eye and shake my head at her, but she was smiling away at Mother Rosario, all charmed that the interview had turned out so well.

I could do without this—and all because I'd burned the porridge.

"Faith, and you won't burn it again," said Da that night when I told him the whole story.

"Is that all the sympathy I get?" I was indignant with him.

"It could be worse," said Da dryly. "You could have landed yourself a job as an assistant gardener to an oul' fella with arthritic knees that'd be ordering you about and making you do all the hardest work."

That wasn't much consolation.

4 *Polly*

Polly laughed when she heard.

Polly was really supposed to be called "Aunty Mary," because she was Mam's sister, but she wouldn't answer to "Aunty." She said it made her feel about a hundred, and she didn't much like "Mary" either. "Too ordinary," she said. "Call me 'Polly.'" Mam said it made her sound like a dairymaid and called her "Mary," as she always had, but I thought "Polly" was much prettier than "Mary."

Really, when I thought about it, Polly was my best friend, and I think I was hers, too. Angela and Nell were good pals, but they were only twelve, like me. Polly was nearly twenty—the height of sophistication—and she was glamorous and full of fun. She wore bright red lipstick and silk stockings and she smoked up the chimney so my mother

wouldn't get the smell, as if she were Polly's mother too, not her older sister. Polly flew around the place, always singing and cracking jokes and cheering everybody up. She dropped into our house most evenings on her way home from Jacob's, the biscuit factory where she worked, and some days she brought a bag of broken biscuits with her and we had a feast.

"Hey, Missus, have you any broken biscuits?" she'd say, flinging the bag of biscuits on the kitchen table.

"Yes!" we chorused. We all knew our line.

"Well, why don't you mend them so?" she'd finish, and we'd all go into kinks of laughter, even though the joke was as old as the hills.

You weren't allowed to take biscuits out of the factory. You could eat as much as you wanted there, but you couldn't take any home. Polly told us that there were random searches of the workers as they left in the evenings, and if you were caught, you were fired, and that was that, so nobody dared to break that rule. But you could buy a bag of broken biscuits very cheaply. The thing was, you never knew what would be in the bag. It was like a lucky dip. It could be Lemon Puffs or Café Noir or Toytown Iced or Kerry Creams, or a mixture. You just didn't know. But we gobbled them all up, regardless. We all loved to hear Polly's laugh on the stairs, because whether or not she had biscuits for us that day, she kept us entertained with gossip about the people she worked with and little incidents that happened: rows between the workers and the bosses, stories about pigeons flying into the biscuit dough, and the practical jokes that the workers would play on the youngest, newest staff members—things like sending them off on daft errands, such as asking the foreman for a bucket of steam.

"Irish dancing, if you don't mind!" Polly laughed again. "Well, you'll be the lovely colleen and no mistake. Flouncing and bouncing you'll be, and kicking up your feet like a hen with fleas."

"I'll give you fleas!" I said with a laugh, but I didn't feel like laughing. I was afraid that those snobby girls, Tess and her friends, would show me up, and that I would make a fool of myself, clumping around on my big, clumsy spaugs. It was all just a big embarrassment as far as I was concerned.

"How's Shamy Macnamara?" I asked, to change the subject. Bringing up the subject of Shamy was a great way to get a rise out of Polly.

"Don't be talking!" said my aunt. "He has me moidhered, so he has."

Shamy Macnamara was "after" Polly. He had set his heart on marrying her, but Polly would have none of it. She always said there wasn't a man in Dublin that was good enough for her and that was a good thing, because then she wouldn't have to marry anyone. She could be her own boss all her life and have her own income, and she wouldn't be worn out having millions of babies either, the way all the other poor women were.

"You and me, Kathleen," she would say, "we'll be

old maids together, won't we? We'll live in a garret and eat chocolates all day long and lounge around in our nightdresses until midday, and we'll paint our toenails red and we won't darn any man's socks for him, will we?"

"We won't!" I would answer delightedly. "We'll be independent women, won't we, Polly?"

"We will. Ladies of leisure. We'll have brandy flips for breakfast and colcannon for tea and we won't call the king our better."

"Except Saturdays," I would interject. On Saturdays, we were going to have tea with sticky buns and cream cakes and chocolate éclairs in Bewley's Café.

Even if Polly had a mind to marry, it wasn't the likes of Shamy Macnamara she'd hitch up with. Shamy didn't take a drink beyond a couple of glasses of Guinness with the lads on a Saturday night, and he was very good to his old mother, but he wasn't very handsome, and he had an annoying way of hanging his head and looking at his feet at the first sign of trouble. Not the sort of hero you'd like to have about the place, as Polly put it.

"Rhett Butler, now there's a man!" Polly said dreamily.

"Would he be anything to the Butlers of Kilkenny?" Da asked, just to annoy her.

"He would not. He's an American in a book I'm reading, and he's a gorgeous man altogether, so he is."

"What book is that?" Da asked.

"*Gone with the Wind*," said Polly dreamily. "I got it out of the circulating library. It's a love story. You wouldn't understand, Tommy Murphy, you old gom, you. The main character is called Scarlett. Isn't that romantic? Scarlett O'Hara."

"O'Hara? Well, now, that's an Irish name too. Would she be anything to—" Da started again.

"Don't!" Polly kicked off her shoes and perched her pretty little stockinged feet, with the dark line of the seam across her toes, up on the mantelpiece. The hem of her dress dipped almost to the floor, and she leaned back and yawned. "Throw us an old Custard Cream, there, Kathleen," she begged.

I complied, and the conversation changed again, this time to my father's chance of work with the nuns.

"They'll have you crawthumping all over the place," Polly warned him, flicking her toes in his direction. "It'll be devotions and missions and novenas and the Lord knows what for you. You'll be destroyed going to church, so you will."

"Going to church never did anyone any harm," said my mother stiffly.

"It's true for you, Alice," said Polly piously, but she winked at me.

It always surprised me to hear my mother being called by her first name. Polly was the only one who used it. The neighbors all called her Mrs. Murphy, and even Da nearly always called her "your mother," when speaking to us children, or "*asthore*" when he addressed her directly. That was because he was from the country.

"Anyway," Polly said quietly to me when the others were talking about something else, "I've bigger fish to fry than Shamy Macnamara."

"Oh! I thought you weren't going to marry anyone at all," I said, remembering our fantasy about the garret and the chocolates and the painted toenails.

"Who mentioned marriage? I'm just talking about

having a bit of fun."

"Oh!" I said again. I wasn't sure about this, but I kept quiet. It wasn't the kind of thing I thought my mam would want to hear about.

"I brought you something," Polly said then.

"I know, the broken biscuits," I said. "Thanks very much."

"No," she said. "Something for yourself."

She slipped a small gold tube into my hand.

"It's only half used," she whispered. "I got a new one, a color that suits me better, but this one is still good. It'll look terrific on you, with your red hair. Dead dramatic."

I looked at the tube. Lipstick. I was too young for lipstick, but I was dying to see what I looked like with it on all the same.

"Come into the bedroom with me," I whispered, and Polly nodded.

"Oh, it wouldn't interest you," she said when Da asked where we were off to.

"Hmm," he said and wagged a finger at her. "Don't you be leading our Kathleen astray, now, Mary."

"Who's Mary?" said Polly, looking all around her with a puzzled look on her face. "I don't see any Marys, do you, Kathleen? Unless you mean your woman up there."

She pointed at a bottle of Lourdes water that my mam kept on the mantelpiece. It was in a beautiful milky white glass bottle in the shape of a statue of the Blessed Virgin. The screw cap was a blue crown with spiky bits and she wore a blue sash down the front of her long white dress.

"You will go straight to hell for blasphemy," said Mam, who'd overheard.

"I will not. It's not blasphemy to say her name is Mary, when it is. I tell you what, if you call me Polly, I won't mention herself at all. Is it a bargain?"

Before Mam could answer, Polly pulled me by the wrist into the bedroom and slammed the door. Then she opened the door again and stuck out her tongue at Mam and gave a giggle. I don't think Mam saw.

"Now, watch me," she said after she'd closed the door again, and I watched.

She stretched her lips and expertly applied a coat of

bright red lipstick. "Geranium, it's called," she said. She didn't bother with a mirror. Then she chomped down on a scrap of newspaper, leaving bright red lip marks like kisses on the margin, and applied the lipstick a second time, this time rolling her lips together to spread the color evenly.

"Your turn," she said and handed me the tube of lipstick.

But I'd changed my mind about wanting to try it.

"No," I said. "Da'll kill me if he sees. I'll try it some day when he's out."

"Out watering the nuns' roses!" said Polly with a giggle, and she flung herself back on our bed, making wide cycling movements with her legs and wriggling her toes inside her stockings.

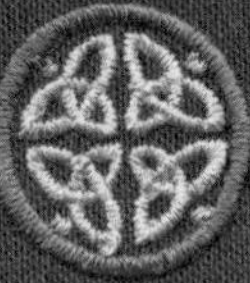

5 *Flying*

I asked Tess and her gang how much the dancing lessons cost. I was hoping they would be too dear, and then I wouldn't have to go.

"Oh, nothing," Tess said. "We pay nothing, do we, girls?"

Brigid began, "Yes, it's free all right—"

Tess tossed her head impatiently and cut across Brigid. "You see, Kathleen?" she said. "It's free. We pay nothing."

I was going to have to tag along with them after school to Mrs. Maguire's Irish Dancing School, whether I liked it or not.

"A new girl!" said Mrs. Maguire, sounding like the spider inviting the fly into her parlor.

She was dumpy and stocky and wore an extraordinary

dress made out of what looked like brown canvas that went down to her ankles.

"She's supposed to look like Queen Maeve in that," Brigid whispered to me. We knew about Queen Maeve, the warrior queen of Connacht who went to war over a bull, because we'd done her in third class.

"She looks like a sack of potatoes," I whispered back, and Brigid got a fit of the giggles.

Mrs. Maguire didn't look as if she could dance a step, and certainly not in that outfit. I never saw her so much as lift a foot, and I soon discovered that all the teaching was done by verbal instructions. So I learned by watching the other, more experienced dancers.

Mrs. Maguire battered out the tunes on a woodwormy old upright piano. Some of the keys were dead, and when she hit one of those, she hummed the note loudly to make up for the missing sound. She mainly played only two tunes: "The Rakes of Mallow" for the reels and "The Irish Washerwoman" for the jigs.

I started with the baby reel.

"*AON, dó, trí, ceathair, cúig, sé, seacht!*" Mrs. Maguire roared over the sound of the piano. That meant ONE, two, three, four, five, six, seven. "*AON, dó, trí, is a hAON, dó, trí.*" ONE, two, three, and a ONE, two, three.

Over and over it went. "*AON, dó, trí, is a hAON, dó, trí.*" Mrs. Maguire kept count. "POINT those toes."

At first, I didn't know what was going on, but I soon got the hang of it. I learned to hold my right foot out precisely in front of my left, with the heel well up, the arch exaggerated, and all my toes clenched so that I seemed to have only a big toe, and that one poised for action, while I counted the opening bars under my breath. Then with a skip, I was off, *AON, dó, trí, ceathair, cúig, sé, seacht, AON, dó, trí, is a hAON, dó, trí*!

I could do it! After a few false starts, something

suddenly clicked, and I was away, starting into action on the *AON* beat like a shot off a shovel, and tripping lightly up to seven. Then I danced the *AON*, *dó*, *trí*, *is a hAON*, *dó*, *trí* on the spot, one leg chasing the other as if I were skipping up an invisible staircase, my skirt bouncing merrily in rhythm with the music, till I came skimming down again in the opposite direction on the next *AON*, *dó*, *trí*, *ceathair*, *cúig*, *sé*, *seacht*.

I loved it. It was like flying. It was better than swinging on the swingboats at the carnival and better than stealing a ride off the milkman's cart by swinging out of the back as it clopped and rolled over the cobbled streets.

I was all hot and sticky at the end of the class and out of breath, but I was thrilled with myself. I could dance!

"I suppose you think you're great, Miss Twinkletoes," said Tess O'Hara, pulling a face at me as we took off our dancing poms and put on our outdoor shoes again. Mrs. Maguire had loaned me a pair of dancing poms because I was new and didn't have my own. They were a bit big for me, but she had given me cardboard insoles to stuff them out.

"No," I said warily, but I knew my eyes were shining with the excitement of it. I couldn't help it. "No, I don't think I'm great at all, but I did enjoy it. Do you not enjoy it, Tess?"

"It's not supposed to be enjoyable," said Tess spitefully. "It's supposed to be a lesson. You are supposed to be learning."

"I am learning," I said humbly. I knew perfectly well that the only way to deal with her was to pretend to flatter her, so I laid it on with a trowel. "I have an awful lot to learn, I know that. It'll be a long time before I'm up to your standard."

"Hmm," said Tess, but she couldn't very well argue with that.

"That'll be ninepence, please," said Mrs. Maguire as I walked past the piano, where she was still sitting, on my way out.

I blushed scarlet. I could feel the blood banging against my temples and my cheeks were radiating heat.

"Ninepence? Oh, I'm sorry, I thought . . ."

"You thought it was free, gratis, and for nothing, did

you?" said Mrs. Maguire huffily. Her face was as red as mine, and she'd drawn in her chin and puffed out her cheeks so that her neck disappeared and she looked like a pigeon or a hen—something fussy with feathers, anyway.

"Well . . ."

"Huh! And how do you think I am supposed to make a living? It's ninepence a lesson or seven-and-six a term, which is twelve lessons. That's a discount of one-and-six if you pay by the lump."

"Seven-and-six?" I'd never even seen seven-and-sixpence all together in one place in my life. My mother certainly wasn't going to be able to fork out that kind of money.

Tess and Annie were tittering away, listening in and pointing and whispering to each other. I blushed even harder, knowing that they were probably laughing at me for not being able to afford the lesson. They were positively rich, compared to me. Ninepence would be nothing to them. They probably got pocket money every week, like children in books. The only pocket money we ever got was when we collected jam jars and took them back to the shop to redeem the deposit on them, a ha'penny a shot.

"I'm sorry, Mrs. Maguire," I mumbled.

"You can bring it next week," she said briskly, closing the lid on the piano and letting her chin jut out again so that her neck reappeared.

"Eh, yes . . . well, no. I . . . don't think I can come next week, I . . ."

"Oh?" said Mrs. Maguire, starting to get all puffy-looking again.

I dropped my voice to a whisper. "Thank you for the lesson," I said, looking over my shoulder. "It was great, but . . . I'll bring you the ninepence as soon as I can. But I can't come again."

Mrs. Maguire stared at me with her mouth open. Her bottom teeth wobbled. I thought they were going to fall out into her lap, but she closed her mouth just in time.

I picked up my navy gabardine raincoat from the bench by the door where all the coats were thrown, and I walked out the door. I didn't look back, but I could hear the stifled giggles of the others.

I ran home through the darkening streets and pounded up the stairs to our rooms, raced through the kitchen and into the girls' bedroom, where I flung myself on the bed and buried my humiliated, scorching face in the cool cotton of the pillowslip.

After a while, my cheeks cooled down and I could bear to lift my head. I took a look in the cracked piece of mirror glass we had propped up on the chest of drawers. My face was bright pink. It didn't go with red hair and freckles. There was a basin of water beside the glass, and I splashed my face with it, pulled the hairbrush through my hair, and went out to face my mother.

"Ninepence!" she said in an outraged voice, as if I were looking for the money for myself. "Ninepence a lesson! Sure I could feed a family on that for a week."

"Ah, Mam," I said wearily. I knew that wasn't true. "Well, it doesn't matter. I didn't much like it anyway. I hate that Tess O'Hara and her pals. I'd just as soon not go again."

"I'm glad to hear it, I'm sure," said my mother, "but I wasn't thinking about how you felt about not going again. I'm still wondering where we're going to get the ninepence for today's lesson."

"Can we not manage just one little ninepence?" I asked in astonishment.

"It might be a little thing to you, my girl, but with your da—"

Just at that point, the door opened and Da came in. He was just coming from his first stint working in the convent gardens.

"Well," he said with a loud sigh, pulling out a chair and flopping into it. "That wasn't so bad, I suppose, and I earned three-and-sixpence for myself, which is no fortune. But it's not to be sneezed at either, and it's an awful lot better than no three-and-sixpence."

He looked very pleased with himself, and he looked from me to my mother and back again, obviously expecting to be congratulated.

"Hand it over," said my mother, stony-faced.

"Huh!" said Da. "Is that the thanks I get?"

But he handed it over all the same.

"Here's ninepence, Kathleen," said my mother. "Run back to Mrs. Maguire's with that now. Never let it be said that the Murphys don't pay their debts. And here's a shilling for yourself, Tommy. Put the rest in the tin box, would you, Kathleen?"

The tin box was an old sweet tin that we kept on the mantelpiece. Mam saved up the rent money in it. It had horses and carriages on it, very swish.

"Sorry, love," said Mam to me, "but you know we can't afford that sort of money."

"I know," I practically shouted. "I don't care about the old dancing. To blazes with Mrs. Maguire and her flipping ninepence anyway. I hope it chokes her."

"Kathleen!" said my mother reproachfully.

But Da took another view. "That's the spirit," he said. "Here's a penny for yourself. Get yourself a fizz bag on the way home."

"Thanks, Da," I said, and I flew out the door and back down the stairs and over the streets to the house where Mrs. Maguire had the long, dingy room that she used for her dancing school.

But it was all my eye. I did care. I did want to dance. And I was good at it, I knew. It was cruel, I thought, that I'd just discovered this lovely thing, only to have it snatched away from me as soon as I got a taste for it. To blazes with Tess O'Hara and her stuck-up pals, too. To blazes with everything!

6 *The Letter*

Of course, it was all over the school by the next morning. Tess O'Hara didn't waste time when she saw a chance to make a fool of someone like me.

"And the best part," Tess had announced, "was that she thought it was free. Free! I mean, what is poor Mrs. Maguire supposed to live on, answer me that? The scratchings of the Murphys' pan? It's free for us, of course, because my daddy works for Guinness's. The same with Annie and Brigid—we're all Guinness families, and always have been. But it's only free because Guinness's pays for it. It's not free to all comers. I mean, you can't just let *anyone* come in off the street and learn for nothing."

Angela and Nell were full of sympathy. Angela said that Nell and herself would hold the skipping rope for me all through *sos* as a special treat. I wouldn't have to hold it for her or Nell at all.

"AON, *dó, trí, ceathair, cúig, sé, seacht*!" they yelled as they turned the rope, turned it and turned it, and I skipped and spun and danced over it, my plaits flying around my shoulders. I was glad I'd put my hair in plaits that day, as it was much easier to skip without my hair flying into my face, even though it meant it would be all crinkly the following day. "AON, *dó, trí, is a h*AON, *dó, trí*."

We had a right laugh, taking off the dancing count. I could see that it annoyed Tess and her pals. Anyway, they made a great show of playing ball, shouting out the bouncing rhyme, "Plainy packet of Rins-o!" as loudly as they could, to drown out the sound of us counting in Irish.

I tried to pretend to myself that I didn't mind. It was true that I wasn't too upset anymore about Tess and the others setting me up like that—I couldn't be bothered with them and their nonsense—but I *did* mind about having to miss the dancing lessons. It wasn't that I wanted what the other girls had. It was the dancing I loved. It was the feeling it gave me—like flying.

Wednesday was Irish dancing day, and by the time the next Wednesday came, I had put it all behind me. I stayed back at school for a while to help with the tidying up. It was Nell's turn to lift back the desk seats on their hinges and sweep the floor and empty the rubbish bins, but we always helped each other when it was our turns. I was just putting on my coat to go home when Brigid Mullane came back into the classroom. She handed me a note.

"It's from Mrs. Maguire," she said. "She wants you back."

I opened the note. It wasn't in an envelope or anything, just folded over, so obviously Brigid had read it on the way back to school from the dancing school. You couldn't blame her. I'd have done the same myself.

Dear Kathleen,
I am prepared to offer you one term's free dancing lessons. You look promising, very light on your feet. If I give you a chance and you do well, maybe your family will be able to see their way to reaching an arrangement with my good self as regards the matter of fees in the future.
Yours faithfully,
Mrs. Margaret Maguire

I couldn't believe it. I stared at Brigid, my mouth hanging open.

"Why?" I asked eventually.

Brigid shrugged. "Mrs. Brady's dancing school won loads of medals at the *feis* last year, and the year before as well. Mrs. Maguire is dying to win more than them this year, but a couple of her best dancers have left. Liz O'Brien was great, but she just sort of . . . disappeared. I'd say old Ma Maguire is looking out for new talent."

"New talent? Me? But I can only do the baby reel."

"Yes, but you're very light on your feet. That's the most important thing."

I wasn't sure what that meant. As far as I knew, I was the same weight on my feet as I was sitting down. I kept staring at Brigid, amazed at what she'd said. She'd never have said anything as nice as that if Tess had been there to overhear.

Nell gave me a thump on the back. "There now, you see, you're great. We always knew it, didn't we, Angie?"

"Close your mouth, Kathleen, or you'll catch flies," said Angela. She was a hearty sort of a soul, but she gave me a big wink and a smile.

"Are you coming so?" asked Brigid, turning to leave the classroom and go back to Mrs. Maguire's place.

"We'll call in to your mam and tell her you'll be late," Angela said, as I hesitated. "Go on, off with you!"

"Thanks," I muttered and, still half dazed, I followed Brigid out of the classroom and down the stairs.

Light on my feet. I'm light on my feet. I kept thinking this all the way over to Mrs. Maguire's, puzzling about what it might mean.

But when we got to class and the music started up, and I counted the opening bars under my breath, waiting for the downbeat for my dance to start, it suddenly came to me. I knew what it meant. The rough, distempered floorboards seemed to disappear from under me, my feet barely brushed them, and I flew. It was all airy and feathery, like walking on water, like skimming over clouds. I was kicking and twirling in a new, airy element, flying in time with the music into a different world, where weight didn't matter, where gravity didn't exist. I wasn't Kathleen Murphy, the poor girl from the tenements with a hole in her stocking and chilblains between her toes, embarrassed by her family's poverty, mocked by Tess O'Hara's gang, and belittled by Sister Eucharia. I was a Celtic princess, and I was going to dance my way to the stars on airy-fairy feet, light as air, free as a bird.

It wasn't always like that, of course. I never again felt quite as airy-footed as on that day when I had my first free dancing lesson. But my love for dancing grew and grew, even though it gradually became more difficult. The steps got more intricate, the order of steps harder to remember, and the music so boring you could scream, as Mrs. Maguire endlessly ground out the same two or three basic tunes, lesson after lesson, until we got our steps foot-perfect and could skip and trip our way through our dances in our sleep.

At home I danced round and round our bedroom as I got dressed in the mornings and wrestled with the tangles in my hair. My sisters threw pillows and shoes at me, shouted, and sang slow tunes like "Red Sails in the Sunset" to put me off the beat—anything to try to get me to stop dancing. But I was like the little girl in the story with the shoes that won't let her be still. My feet were enchanted. I didn't climb the stairs, I danced up them; I didn't walk across a room, I danced across it. Even in bed at night, my feet twitched as I went over the steps in my head. When that happened, Patsy and Lily grabbed my toes from the other end of the bed and tickled the soles of my feet, till I nearly choked and had to promise to stop. But always, even when making my best effort to keep my feet still, I danced in my head, listening to a tune only I could hear.

7 *A Plan*

By the middle of that term, I could do slip jigs, sailor's hornpipes, hard reels—the lot. I learned fast because I loved it, and the more difficult the steps got, the greater the effort I put in to master them. The hornpipe was my favorite. We wore hard shoes for the hornpipe, and I loved both the leisurely pace and the rap of my hard shoes on the boards. It was nearly like tap dancing, and you could let your body go loose and let all the energy drain down into your feet, instead of having to keep the top half of yourself completely rigid, the way you had to in order to get the kicks and rocks right in the jigs.

Tess O'Hara teased me and mocked me every chance she got. I think she was jealous because I was doing so well, even though I was new to it all. Every

now and again Mrs. Maguire would thump down on the piano keys with her arms, right up to the elbows, making a terrible crashing sound. Everyone would stop, with their feet in the air, and she would yell out, as if in pain, "Tess O'HARA! Will you PLEASE leave Kathleen Murphy ALONE!" But I would only give a little smile. I'd got used to Tess and her carrying on, so that in the end I didn't even notice it anymore, the way you get used to flies in the summertime or chilblains in the winter.

Mrs. Maguire had picked her team for the *feis* by now, and I was one of the first to get a place on it. She said she relied on me to do well, *chun glóire Dé agus onóra na hÉireann*, which means "to the glory of God and the honor of Ireland." That made me nervous and proud at the same time—the honor and glory bit—but I nodded and said I would do my best.

Brigid was being entered in the *feis* too, but Mrs. Maguire said she wasn't sure that Tess and Annie were up to scratch. She'd give them a chance to prove themselves over the next few weeks, she said, but she'd have to see. Tess and Annie muttered a lot about that. They said Mrs. Maguire had it in for them. They said she only entered people she thought would win medals. They glared at me when they said that, as if something was my fault, but I have to say I thought that made perfect sense. What was the point of cluttering up the competitions with people who hadn't a hope?

Just as we were leaving on the day she announced the *feis* entrants, Mrs. Maguire made another announcement that sent my heart down into my boots.

"Now, *a chailíní,*" she said, "I want you all to make sure your mothers get you the finest Irish dancing costumes in Dublin for the *feis*. When Maguire girls get up on that stage, I want you all looking absolutely splendid. No ankle socks, please, they only get baggy and dirty. You are all young ladies now, and black lisle stockings is what I want to see, and nice costumes, green if possible. That's the most appropriate color for Irish girls, being the color of Our Native Land. A dress, knee length or a little shorter, with Celtic decoration, and a *brat*, of course. I have Maguire School of Irish Dancing pins that I have had specially made in the style of the beautiful Tara brooch, and I will lend every girl two of these to pin her *brat* to the shoulders of her dress, so that you will go out there wearing the insignia of your dancing school and a symbol of Old Ireland. But your costumes, of course, are your own responsibility. *Ceist ag éinne?*"

That last bit meant "Any questions?" But everyone else had been in *feiseanna* before and didn't need to ask. I was the only one who was new to it, and I didn't dare ask anything.

"Well," said Tess O'Hara with a smirk at me as we clattered down the stairs from Mrs. Maguire's room. "So now!"

She didn't say any more. She didn't need to.

She knew perfectly well that I didn't have a hope in the wide world of getting hold of a dancing costume that would be good enough to wear representing Mrs. Maguire, not to mention God and Ireland, at the *feis*. And I knew she was right.

I stumbled home, going over and over in my mind what Mrs. Maguire had said, trying to find some solution to this costume problem. By the time I got to our front door, I had made my decision. I would say nothing to my mother about the *feis* or the dancing costume. It would only annoy and upset her, and I didn't know which would be worse. I wouldn't say anything about it to anyone just yet. But I had a plan. I wasn't sure if it would work, but it was the best I could think of.

8 *The Conversion of Russia*

Sister Eucharia was a great one for miracles. She had a special devotion to Saint Bernadette of Lourdes, who was only a new saint. She told us that we should all be great followers of Bernadette, because she was a girl, just like us. She meant a poor girl, but of course she couldn't exactly put it like that. Brigid Mullane put up her hand and said she thought Saint Bernadette had been a nun, so how could she be a girl?

Sister Eucharia got very angry, even though it was a fair question. We knew when "Yuki," as we called her, was angry, because little bubbles appeared at either side of her mouth. That was always a sure sign. I think Yuki thought Brigid was giving cheek, but I could tell from the way she asked that she only wanted to know. After all, everyone was a girl once, or a boy, so what was so special about Saint Bernadette having been a girl? Grown-ups just didn't like it when children asked questions. I never understood that, because they were always asking us questions.

"She became a nun in later life," Sister Eucharia said in a very clipped voice, but that didn't really answer Brigid's question. Either she was a girl or she was a grown-up—she couldn't be both. But sure enough, all the statues showed her as a young girl, a bit older than ourselves maybe, though it's hard to tell with statues—the faces are so dead. Every statue had her kneeling down with a pile of *brosna* at her feet, as if she was about to make a fire.

Anyway, Sister Eucharia told us that to become a saint, you have to work miracles. People have to pray to you and then you work your miracle, and then the Pope says you can be a saint. That's how it works. My mam was a great believer in miracles, too. She swore she'd got that job in the convent garden for my da by doing the First Fridays. I didn't have time to do the First Fridays—that takes nine months—but I could do one of those quick novenas, the ones you do over nine days instead of over nine months or nine weeks.

Sister Eucharia was very impressed to find me in the convent chapel every morning before school, lighting candles to Saint Bernadette. I'd picked on Bernadette because of the poor girl connection, and I suppose Sister Eucharia had influenced me in that direction, too. Anyway, there was a little indoor grotto to Our Lady of Lourdes built into an alcove in the chapel. It included Saint Bernadette, and it was a nice place to light candles. It smelled of cold stone and candle grease.

Also, I figured that if Saint Bernadette was only a new saint, she must have had practice recently at doing miracles, so she might be a better bet than one of the older saints, who might have forgotten how. I did an awful lot of jam-jar hunting, so that I was able to put a penny in the box every morning for the candles at the grotto. By the time I had my novena finished, I would have spent ninepence. That seemed a satisfactory amount, because it was what a dancing lesson would cost if I had to pay for it. It seemed like a sort of sign that I was doing the right thing.

"What are you doing, child?" Sister Eucharia asked me on the first morning.

"I'm doing a novena to Saint Bernadette, Sister."

Sister Eucharia frowned. I had thought she'd be pleased. But when she saw that I was sticking to it, and that I was in there morning after morning, she began to soften up.

By day six there was still no sign of a dancing costume at the foot of my bed, as I expected there would be, like a present from Santy on Christmas morning. So I decided I'd up the ante. I told God, through Saint Bernadette, that if He sent me a dancing costume, I would be good forever and ever.

Day seven dawned, and there was still no sign of the dancing costume.

On day eight, I made the supreme sacrifice, since that's what God seemed to be holding out for. I promised God that if He sent me a dancing costume, I would be a nun when I grew up, just like Saint Bernadette. I felt sure that would clinch it. It wouldn't be all that difficult, I thought, because I didn't mean to get married anyway. I was going to be an old maid in a garret with Polly. I thought I could do that for a few years, and then I would enter the convent. That seemed a fair sort of arrangement.

On day nine, I was very disappointed when the dancing costume didn't appear. There was always the chance, of course, that God was waiting for me to do the last day of the novena before showing His hand, so I got up as usual and went to the chapel to light my daily candle to Saint Bernadette. Old Yuki came up to me again, and she asked me what I was praying for so hard. Was somebody in my family sick?

"No, Sister," I whispered. "I'm praying for a dancing costume to wear in the *feis*."

Sister Eucharia's mouth started to bubble like a porridge saucepan on the range. She stared at me, her unnaturally white face seeming to get even whiter. I couldn't work out what I'd done. I hadn't spoken aloud, had I? No, I felt sure I had whispered.

At last she got a few words out, though she seemed to find it difficult to talk.

"You, you . . . you bold strap, you!" she practically shouted at me.

She caught me by the elbow, yanked me up from where I was kneeling in front of the grotto, and steered me out of the chapel into the corridor outside, where she could yell at me. She shook me good and hard and she kept calling me a bold strap.

"But . . . but, Sister," I managed to get out, "what's wrong? You said Saint Bernadette was good for miracles."

"Miracles are a sacred gift from God, girl. If you ask for a miracle, it should be for some worthy purpose, such as healing a sick person or . . . or . . . or the Conversion of Russia."

"The Conversion of Russia, Sister?" I'd never heard of this. "Why would I ask for a thing like that?"

"Why wouldn't you?" She shook me again. "Call yourself a Christian, do you? And you are happy to see Russia languishing in paganism and communism? I suppose maybe you'd like to see those revolutionaries winning out in Spain, too, would you? It would suit you better to be praying for our lads going out there to help General Franco, so it would."

"Spain?" I said in bewilderment. "General Who?"

The only thing I knew about Spain was that that's where the oranges came from. But Sister Eucharia had lost interest in Spain.

"You should be ashamed of yourself, wasting good prayers on Irish dancing costumes. What sort of a pagan ritual is that, anyway, Irish dancing?"

"It's not, Sister, it's not!" I insisted. "Mother Rosario loves it. She says it's 'very appropriate' for Irish girls."

Sister Eucharia dropped my elbow, which she had been gripping and squeezing all this time.

"Get away with you to your classroom, and don't let me catch you praying for . . . for . . . trivialities ever again. I wouldn't be surprised if God was very angry with you, making light of holy religion like that."

I was glad it was the ninth day and I'd finished my novena. I certainly wouldn't want to meet Sister Eucharia in the convent chapel again. I hoped that by the time I entered the convent, Sister Eucharia would be dead.

Then I realized that was a dreadful thing to hope for, so I changed it to retired.

9 *Miracles*

The next morning I hardly dared to open my eyes. The full nine days were up, I'd made my enormous promise—surely God couldn't fail to answer my prayers. I lay there and willed a costume to be on the bed.

Eventually, Madge leaned over and prised one of my eyelids open.

"I thought you had died in the night," she said when I pushed her hand away. "You're usually up so early these days."

I didn't tell her that the reason I wasn't getting up early that morning was that I'd finished my novena. "No fear I'd die on you," I said, sitting up and glancing casually around the room.

No sign of the dancing costume. How could that be?

Could Sister Eucharia be right? Could God be angry with me for asking for such a trivial thing? But surely God would understand how important it was to me. I counted on God being more broad-minded than Sister Eucharia.

Maybe it was more serious than that. Maybe it was that God didn't want me for a nun. Maybe He thought I wasn't worthy.

Worse than that, though, the *feis* was in three weeks' time, and I still had no costume and no sign of one. With a heavy heart, I started to get dressed. I didn't think much of Saint Bernadette as a miracle worker, and I decided to cut her out of my prayers altogether from now on. *Anyway*, I thought, *any friend of old Yuki's can't be much of a saint*.

I dragged myself into the kitchen for breakfast, disappointment weighting my feet. Mam was ladling out the porridge.

"Kathleen!" she said. Not "Good morning, did you sleep well?" Just "Kathleen!"

I looked up at her. Was I in some sort of trouble? I didn't much care, to tell the truth. I felt as if I already had so much to worry me, a bit of bother with my mother would wash over me and leave me unaffected.

"Kathleen, I hear you were picked for the *feis*, and you never told me a thing about it. Aren't you the great girl, all the same!"

Mam was beaming away at me. I wasn't sure how to react, but I chanced a little smile.

"Why didn't you say anything, love?"

"Well," I said. "Well . . ."

"Now, you probably haven't thought of this," said Mam, not waiting for my answer, "but you know, you will need a dancing costume for this *feis*. They get all dolled up in those Gaelic League clothes, these Irish dancers, with harps and shamrocks and goodness knows what. We'll have to make sure you're as well dressed as the rest of them."

My heart rose. My mam was all on for it. She didn't seem worried about the expense. I should have told her in the first place and saved myself the novena and the row with old Yuki and all the worry, not to mention pledging myself to the convent.

"Now, this is what we'll do," said Mam, all business. "I'm going to go over to Frawley's this morning and see if they have any remnants that would do for your costume. Stand up there till I have a look at you and see how much I'll need."

I stood up on a chair, and she turned me round and took the measure of me with her eye.

"I wonder would six yards do it?" she asked herself. "There's the . . . what do you call the shawly thing?"

"The *brat*," I said.

"The *brat*, and then the skirt has to be full—pleats, I suppose, or half pleats; that's very sore on material. But if I cut it very carefully, I'd say I'd get away with six yards."

I was beaming away by this stage, delighted with the way things were turning out. It was like a miracle.

Suddenly, it struck me. It *was* a miracle. This was God's way of answering my prayers. I should have realized He wasn't going to send me a beautiful costume out of nowhere, by magic. That sort of thing only happened in stories. It was a very childish idea to think that He would work like that. This was His way of getting me a costume.

The only problem now was that I was going to have to go through with my side of the bargain and be a nun when I grew up. Maybe I should have held my fire. Maybe if I'd just told Mam about my problem in the first place, I wouldn't have needed a miracle. I'd probably signed away my life for nothing.

Well, this was no time to be worrying about that. It was time to be planning my costume. I was going to be gorgeous. Mam would see to that. I was in safe hands.

10 *Bad News*

I rushed home from school that day, to see if Mam had got the material for the costume.

"No," she said, "not yet. But I found just the thing. It's a lovely soft light wool, sky blue—it'll be perfect."

"Blue!" I said. "Mam, dancing costumes are supposed to be green."

"Green? Do they have to be green?"

"No, they don't have to be, I suppose, but everyone else will be in green. Or yellow—they're yellow sometimes."

"Well, then, you'll be different. Oh, it really is a lovely shade of blue, you'll see."

"Why didn't you buy it so?" I asked. "Were you waiting for me to see it?"

"Yes, but that's not the only reason. The thing is, it's

not a remnant. There was nothing suitable in the remnant bin. I looked in a few places, but I kept coming back to this lovely material in Frawley's. It's too dear, though, at full price."

My heart dropped. What was the point in building me up like this if there wasn't going to be a costume after all?

"But the thing is," Mam went on, "the bolt of fabric is nearly finished. If just one more person buys the makings of a dress, the remainder will be too short to sell off the bolt, and they'll have to put it in the remnant bin. The trick is to be quick off the mark and snaffle it as soon as it appears."

"How will we manage that, Mam?" I asked.

"You'll have to keep an eye out," Mam said. "You'll have to come home the long way from school every day and check on it. As soon as it appears in the remnant bin, I want you to race home to me and I'll be up with the money to buy it."

"But Mam, suppose there isn't six yards in it?"

"Ah, there will be," said Mam. "God is good."

God is very good at keeping a person in suspense,

I thought to myself, but I didn't say a word. I thought maybe I should start praying that there'd be enough material left in the remnant, but then I decided I'd got myself into enough trouble with prayers and novenas, and this time, maybe I'd just wait and see.

I did as my mam said, and I came around by Thomas Street every day on the way home, but still the bolt of sky blue material stayed on the shelf. Mam was right, it was really lovely, so I didn't even mind that it wasn't green. But nobody seemed to want to buy any of it. Maybe it was too dear for everyone, not just for us.

One evening, Mam went to bed early. She thought she had a cold coming on. I was going to have to get up early and do the breakfast, she said. She didn't think she'd be able to do it.

I promised faithfully that this time I wouldn't burn the porridge. Mam showed me how to pull out the damper more gently and then edge it back a bit, once the fire got going, so I was more in control of the heat.

I managed the porridge fine, and I brought a bowl of it in to Mam, where she lay in bed. She shook her head and pushed my hand away.

"No, love," she said, and then she went into a fit of coughing. "Thanks," she said when she got her breath back, "but I couldn't touch it."

"Feed a cold, Mam," I said. "That's what you always say."

"And starve a fever," she said. "I think it's more than a cold, love. I think I'm getting something."

"Poor Mam," I said. "Will you have a cup of tea?"

"I will," she said. "You're a great girl, Kathleen."

I loved it when she said I was a great girl, even if I didn't always think it was true.

"Mam," I said when I brought her in the tea, "what ever happened to Liz O'Brien?" It was making the porridge again that brought it all back to me, I suppose.

"Ah, you know what happened to her, poor girl."

"I don't, Mam. Did she die?"

"Die! Of course she didn't die. Sure if she'd died, there'd've been a funeral. No. She was in a bad way. We thought for sure the childbed fever had got her, but I brought her through, I'm proud to say."

"But Mam, she's disappeared."

"She went to England, Kathleen, to get away from the wagging tongues."

"What wagging tongues, Mam?"

"The ones that think a poor girl who has a baby and no husband to show for it is a bad girl."

"So she went to England with her baby?"

"Ah no, sure how could she get work if she had a baby with her? She gave the baby to the nuns, and off she went."

"To the nuns!" I was horrified. "Nuns don't have babies."

"No, but they find good homes for poor babies like that."

This was news to me, but I didn't ask any more. Obviously, there were more important things in the world than Mrs. Maguire's chances of a haul of medals in the *feis*, but I didn't think I wanted to know any more about them just now. It was just too sad to think about, people having to give their babies away.

The days dragged on, and still my mam wasn't

getting any better, and still the sky blue material sat there. The man in the fabric department was getting to know me by now, since I stopped every day to check on it.

"Are you going to buy that material or not?" he asked me one day, and I plucked up the courage to tell him the whole story.

He laughed when he heard it—I put in the bit about Saint Bernadette and everything—and he said that as soon as the last person bought fabric off the bolt, he'd hide it behind the counter and keep the remnant for me.

He had a gold tooth and it gleamed when he smiled. I thought that meant he must be very rich. He had a gold watch, too, in his top pocket. Very smart he looked, tall and with dark eyes and hair. He looked much too nice to be working in a shop. He should have been something much more stylish, I thought, like a headwaiter or the conductor of a band or an ambassador. I had this idea of an ambassador in my head, a handsome man with epaulettes and a sword who bowed a lot to ladies.

"Oh, thank you!" I said. "Thank you very much. You're a saint."

"Get away out of that," he said, just like my da. "But I have a little daughter myself, and I know how hard it can be sometimes when you want something very badly."

I felt a bit better after that, but I really thought God was making heavy weather of this miracle. Maybe I was like Job in the Bible and He was trying my patience. I certainly felt like telling Him what to do with His sky blue fabric, but I didn't. I let on to be all sweetness and light and just kept hoping I would come by one day from school and the fabric would have disappeared off its place on the shelf, and then I would know that my friend in the fabric department had hidden the remnant for me.

One morning when I went in to Mam with her cup of tea, she was much worse. Her eyes were staring, and there was sweat running off her face into her hair, which was wringing wet on the bolster. When I spoke, she didn't answer. I got an awful fright. I ran out to get Da, and he came into the room and shook her till her teeth rattled, and still she only stared and said nothing.

"Run for Mrs. O'Brien, Kathleen," he said. "And then take those children off to school. Eddy, Eddy, what'll we do with Eddy? Run over to Mrs. Conlon after you've called on Mrs. O'Brien, and ask her could she mind him for the day."

I didn't need to be told twice. I flew for Mrs. O'Brien. She was an old friend of my mam's, and her children were all grown up, except Jimmy, and even he was nearly fourteen. She'd be able to come and sit all day with my mam if she was needed. Mrs. Conlon was a good friend, too. She lived in the same house as us, and my mam had delivered all her children. Eddy would be fine with her, as he'd have children his own age to play with.

Mrs. O'Brien threw her coat on over her apron and ran with me to our house, up the stairs, and straight into my mother's bedroom.

"Boil the kettle, Kathleen," she said as she closed

the door. "Who's minding Eddy?" she asked, sticking her head out again.

"Mrs. Conlon," said Madge. "Is Mam going to die?"

"Devil a bit of it," said Mrs. O'Brien. "She's a hardy soul."

She came out after a minute and said, "She's fine, she's fine."

We were all sitting on the stairs, my sisters and I, with our schoolbags on. We were afraid to go to school in case something dreadful happened.

"There, now," I said to the others, "you've heard what Mrs. O says. Mam's going to be grand, and the best thing we can do now for her is go off to school and keep out of the way."

Mrs. O'Brien gave me a little wink, and I knew I'd said the right thing, but I also knew she was lying and that Mam wasn't fine at all.

Even so, I came around by Frawley's on my way home that evening. Partly habit, partly because I was half afraid to go home. When I got as far as the shop and looked in the big plate glass window, my heart did a little skip. The blue fabric was no longer in its place on the shelf. That meant someone must have bought a length off it and my friend the ambassador, as I called him to myself, was saving the remnant for me. I'd have to go home quick and ask Mam for the money.

But Mam was sick, dying maybe. What sort of a daughter was I, thinking about dress material at a time like this? I walked slowly past the shop, willing myself to keep going, not to let my feet take me in at the doorway.

What's the point? I thought to myself then, when I'd got beyond the shop. *I may as well find out about the material now that I'm here. It isn't going to do my mam any harm, and sure, maybe by the time I get home, she'll be much better.*

So I turned back and went into Frawley's. I pushed the door and the bell rang loudly. The ambassador looked up and smiled when he saw me, his gold tooth glinting in the light. Then his expression changed.

"Bad news, Kathleen," he said sorrowfully.

My mother! Dead—I knew it! He must have heard from the neighbors. My head pounded with dread.

"The last person who came in bought a whole lot

of that lovely blue material," he went on. "There's only three-quarters of a yard left, so it wouldn't do you."

"Oh!" I said, and something suddenly seemed to fill my throat, and I couldn't say anything more.

My mother wasn't dead; it was only that the material had been sold. But it still seemed as if something dreadful had happened. Everything was all mixed up in my mind—the material, Mam being sick, the *feis*, the money, Tess O'Hara's gloating face when she discovered I wasn't going to be able to dance in the *feis* because I had no costume, and Liz O'Brien and her baby. I felt as if my head were going to burst. Sister Eucharia was probably right. God didn't like the way I'd prayed for a costume and this was His way of punishing me. I wasn't going to get my costume, and it was my fault that my mam was sick, too.

I felt tears on my face. I rubbed them quickly with my fists, but the ambassador noticed.

He said, "Ah, now, it's not that serious, love."

"It is!" I sobbed, and I ran out of the shop and dashed home.

11 *Scarlett O'Hara*

As I ran, I made a new bargain with God. I told Him I was sorry for praying for a dancing costume. I said I'd pray for the Conversion of Russia next, but right now what I needed was for my mam to get better. If He would only make my mam better, I'd forget all about the costume and the *feis*. I'd give up dancing altogether, even. I'd stay at home on Wednesday afternoons and help my mam to do the mending.

When I got home, Polly was there, sprinkling sugar on their bread for the little ones. They were all home from school before me, because I had gone around by Frawley's.

"Polly!" I shouted as soon as I saw her, and I flung myself into her arms.

"My, my," said Polly, "I know you're fond of me,

Kathleen, but you're all over me like a big sheepdog. You're worse than my Bill. Will you stand back a minute till I get my breath!"

"Sorry," I said with a gulp, and I sat down at the kitchen table. I pushed aside a slice of bread and butter and folded my arms on the table. Then I put down my head on my arms and I had a good cry. The little ones just sat and watched me.

"There, there," Polly kept saying to me in a low voice, to calm me.

She stopped saying it for a minute, to whoosh the younger ones out to play on the street. She put Madge in charge and told them to be home by seven o'clock, when she'd have their tea ready for them.

"There, there," she said to me again. "She's going to

be all right. Mrs. O'Brien called the Jubilee nurse. She said your ma is going to be fine. We won't have to send her away to a sanatorium or anything. We just have to look after her, keep her warm, and give her healthy food, that's all. She'll be fine, Kathleen, you'll see."

I looked up. A sanatorium was where they sent you if you got tuberculosis, or "TB," as we always called it. TB was a killer disease, and everyone dreaded it. You couldn't even mention the word.

"Sanatorium?" I screeched at Polly. "That means—"

"No!" said Polly. "I just said no sanatorium. She's going to be all right."

I couldn't work out whether my mother actually had TB or not. You couldn't ask a question like that outright. It was worse than mentioning childbirth. If you didn't get sent to the sanatorium, you were supposed to be put into isolation, so the rest of the family wouldn't catch it, but there wasn't a ghost of a chance of isolating a sick person where we lived.

"But if we don't send her to the sanatorium, she'll die!" I cried.

"I keep telling you, lovey," said Polly gently. "She's

not dying, she's getting better. We are all going to look after your mam and fatten her up and get her well again. She's the most popular woman in Pimlico. Sure, she delivered half the neighborhood. Three of the neighbors have been around already with beef tea and barley water and the devil knows what, and a relic of Father Charles from Mount Argus to put under her pillow. She's well looked after and she's going to get better. We'll all pray like mad, and she'll be fine."

"Pray!" I said, and that set me off again. I was sick of praying, and look where it had got me!

"How come you were so late home?" Polly asked. She didn't really want to know, I knew that. She was just trying to think of something to talk to me about, to stop me crying.

I dried my eyes and I told her about the material in Frawley's, about how I'd been watching it every day, but now it was gone, and I wasn't going to be able to have my costume after all.

"It's just as well," she said, tossing her hair. "You couldn't have got up on the stage in a sky blue costume—you'd have made a holy show of yourself.

I don't know what your mam was thinking of. She must have been sickening at the time. Dancing costumes are green, everyone knows that."

"That's what I thought," I said, "but she had me convinced this would be lovely, and it *was* lovely material, Polly. Oh, it was so gorgeous, and now I will have no costume, but I don't want one anyway, with Mam so sick; I just want her better." And I was off again, in a fit of crying.

Polly stroked my hair for a while, and after I calmed down a bit, she started to chuckle softly.

"What have you got to laugh about?" I asked crossly.

"I'm after having an idea. Wait till you hear it—it's the best idea in the world!"

"What?" I asked.

"You know that book I'm reading?"

"No," I said sullenly. How could I know what she was reading?

"I told you about it. The one with Scarlett O'Hara in it. *Gone with the Wind*."

"Don't mention O'Haras to me," I said bitterly, thinking of Tess. "And who's Bill?" I asked suddenly.

I remembered that she'd mentioned someone called Bill earlier. I'd never heard of him before now.

"Bill, if you must know, is a person I am walking out with, and he's the handsomest man that ever walked on shoe leather. He has big broad shoulders and his dark, dark eyes smolder. He's just like Mr. Rhett Butler in the story."

"Oh!" I said, startled by Polly's enthusiasm.

"But do you want to hear my brilliant idea, or would you rather hear about my love life? Because I can't talk about two things at the same time."

"What's your idea, then?"

"In the story, Scarlett needs a fancy outfit, but she has no money."

"Mmm?" I said. I was beginning to see that there might be a connection.

"So what she does is this. She lives in a gorgeous big house—"

"I thought you said she had no money."

"The family used to be rich, but they lost—but listen, that doesn't matter. The point is this. She needed an outfit, she had no money, but she had a brain wave. She eyed up the lovely velvet curtains they had in the fancy big drawing room of their mansion, and quick as a flash she had them off the window and made up into a beautiful gown with a matching muff and the cutest little hat you ever saw."

I stared at her. My brain was moving slowly.

"We haven't got any fancy velvet curtains," I said. "We only have blinds."

"But *I* have! *We* have," she practically shouted. "Not velvet. We have lovely green wool curtains at home. I made them last year when Pat won a bit of money on the horses and gave me some for myself. I was tired of the wind coming whistling through that front window, so I made some lovely wool curtains with heavy lining to keep the draught out."

Polly lived nearby with another uncle and aunt of ours who had no children. They had a nice little house, and they always seemed rich to me, though really it was just that they weren't quite as poor as we were.

"But you need them," I said. "You just said, they're to keep the draught out."

"Not at all, sure I can hang the lining. It's really the

lining that does the trick."

"No, Polly, I couldn't. I couldn't let you take down your lovely curtains to make me a dancing costume."

"You don't have to let me," said Polly with a shrug. "I can do it without your permission. They're my curtains. I made them myself. I can do what I like with them."

Suddenly I got a fit of laughing.

"What?" said Polly. She always loved a laugh. "What's the big joke?"

"Sister Eucharia," I said. "She told me God would be cross with me for praying for a dancing costume. She had me promising God I would pray for the Conversion of Russia instead. She had me promising not to bother about the dancing costume, to give up dancing altogether. If she heard I was going to the *feis* dressed up in a pair of curtains you made with money Uncle Pat won on the horses . . ."

Polly laughed too, and then we had a hug, and after that, we wet a fresh pot of tea for my mam. I took a cup in to her, and she was looking a lot better. Very pale, very tired, her eyes huge in her head, but she was able to talk a little bit, and she said in a whispery little voice, "What are you and Polly laughing about out there? Do you not know you have a dying woman in the house?"

"Mam!" I said. "Don't talk like that, even in a joke!" But I was delighted that she was well enough to make a joke.

"I'm that pleased to get a proper cup of tea," Mam said, her voice still very soft and weak. "I'm blue in the face drinking beef tea. It's terrible stuff, you know, but it's supposed to keep your strength up."

"Why do communists drink beef tea?" asked Polly, coming in behind me.

I didn't know what she was at. She must be on about the Conversion of Russia again.

"Do they?" I said.

"Because proper tea is theft," she said, and she collapsed on my mam's bed in a fit of the giggles.

"Ouch!" protested Mam. "Will you get off me? You're sitting on my bunions."

"Sorry, I'm an awful elephant," Polly said, moving farther down on the bed, away from Mam. "Proper tea, *property*—get it? Bill told me that one. He's a great intellectual, you know."

Mam gave a faint little smile. I hadn't a clue what the joke was, but I was so delighted to see Mam smiling that I broke out in a big beaming smile myself.

"What's an intellectual?" I asked.

"Something to make busy people talk," Mam said.

That was another one of those things she said when she didn't want to answer a question. It was just typical of her. She must be feeling better to be back to that sort of talk. Maybe she really was going to be all right.

12 *Cottage Industry*

Polly was as good as her word. Next evening she brought one of the curtains around, and she draped it over me to see how it suited me.

"Terrific," she said. "You're pure gorgeous. With that hair, green is perfect. I told you you'd make a lovely colleen."

My da thought we were both mad, trying to make a dress out of a pair of curtains.

"Not mad, Tom," said Polly, laying the curtain across the kitchen table and flashing away with her big, sharp cutting shears. "Enterprising. Your friend Mr. de Valera would be proud of us, producing homespun dancing costumes, as good as. Sure, we're a proper little cottage industry, so we are."

Da snorted, pretending to be irritated, but I could

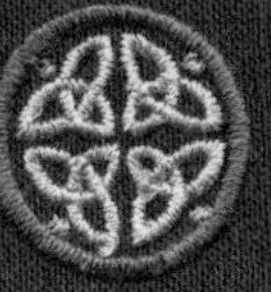

see that he was really trying to stifle a laugh.

By the end of the evening, the structure of the dress was in place, held together with pins and bits of tissue paper and little things marked on it with white thread. I didn't really follow it all, because I'm terrible at dress-making. I never got past an awful apron that I had to make at school. It was so bad that my mother cut it up for dusters.

"Can you embroider?" Polly asked as she poked away at the waist, trying to make the pleats gather in neatly.

"No," I said. "Can you?"

"No," she said, "but we'll cross that bridge when we come to it. Do you know, I could murder for a fag. Do you think your mother would smell it?"

All the girls of Polly's age smoked, but Mam was old-fashioned about it. She said it was common, and she didn't like Polly doing it.

"Of course she would," I said, "but I'd say she's past caring."

Mam was no worse, but she was no better either. She still coughed a lot. She seemed to have got stuck at a certain level of illness. It was as if all her strength had been sapped away, and without it she couldn't make the effort to get well again.

"It's an ill wind that blows nobody any good," Polly said, and she pulled a cigarette out of her handbag. The cigarette was a bit battered looking, but it was intact. I loved Polly's handbag. You never knew what might come out of it. This time, she brought out a Lemon's toffee with the cigarette and handed the toffee to me.

"Give us a light there, Tom," she said to my da.

He took a twist of paper and lifted the hot plate off the range to light it. Then he held it out to her, and she bent her head to catch the light.

She closed her eyes with pleasure on the first puff,

and then sat there dreamily smoking her cigarette, as if she were someplace else entirely. Suddenly she looked around, found a saucer, and quenched the cigarette.

"Are you saving it?" I asked. I'd seen people do that, smoke only half a cigarette so they'd have the other half for another time.

"No," she said. "I just don't feel like it anymore. I've got a lot on my mind." Then she stopped, as if I wasn't there. She put her hand over her forehead and sat back in her chair with her eyes closed.

She was acting so strange, I was terrified, sure she had caught the TB off Mam.

"Polly?" I whispered after a minute or two. "Are you all right, Polly?"

My da hadn't noticed any of this. He was reading the evening paper.

"Right as rain," said Polly, opening her eyes and smiling at me. "It's nothing, I'm fine. Make a drop of tea, Kathleen, love, and I'll get on with this sewing."

13 *Celtic Knots*

The night before the *feis*, Polly sewed the last stitches on the costume. She sat back and admired her work. "Now then, Kathleen, get yourself inside of that, quick march."

I gathered up the dress. The wool was thick and soft, and I could hear a quiet crinkling sound as I smoothed down the skirt. Polly had inserted a piece of stiff lining at the waist, "to give it a bit of body," she said.

"Thanks, Polly," I said, and I went into the bedroom to try it on.

I came out again in a minute, to show Polly.

"You're lovely, Kathleen," she said, riffling my hair. "That's your color. You should always wear it."

Madge and Lily and Patsy all gathered around and patted me down, and I smiled, wriggling a bit inside

the dress, getting used to the feel of it. Even Eddy pointed and said, "Kat!"

"It's a lovely color on you," Polly said again, "but it's a pity it's so plain. A little shamrock or something would have been nice, but sure, we can't have everything."

"Thanks, Polly," I said again. I didn't mind not having a shamrock.

Polly picked up the *brat* then, which she had lined with a piece of the saffron silk casing of my mother's best wedding-present eiderdown. At Mam's urging, Polly had cut a large square out of the underside and patched the hole with a piece of cotton sheeting, and Mam said you'd never know. I suppose you wouldn't as long as you didn't turn the eiderdown upside down, but it looked pretty peculiar underneath all the same.

"I like this best," said Lily, stroking the slippery lining of the *brat*. Yellow was her favorite color. "Could I have a *brat*, Polly?"

"When you're big," said Polly, "and if you're good."

"I'll tell you what," I said to Lily. "I have a tiny rag doll that has no clothes. If you asked very nicely, I'd say Polly could run up a little frock out of the scraps of that yellow material, and you could put it on the rag doll. Would you like that? Would you do it, Polly?"

Polly nodded, and Lily did a little skip of excitement.

I had the two Tara pins that Mrs. Maguire had given me, and we pinned the *brat* to the shoulders of the dress. Polly turned back a slip of the *brat* so that the glorious saffron yellow of the lining showed, and I did a little skip of excitement myself, just like Lily. I grabbed my youngest sister's hands then, and the two of us jigged up and down the kitchen, me trying to get used to the way the dress fell against my knees.

"AON, *dó, trí, is a h*AON, *dó, trí*," sang Patsy.

"A touch of that Geranium lipstick, now, and you'd

be the belle of the ball," said Polly. "Where did you put it at all?"

"No!" I yelped. "Irish dancers don't wear lipstick, Polly! It's not the cha-cha I'm doing. Do you want Mrs. Maguire to have my guts for garters?"

I went in to Mam, then, to show her. She was sitting up with her pillow tucked in behind her for support. I hadn't seen her sitting up since the day she got sick.

"Look at me, Mam!" I said, and I did a little twirl.

"You're a vision, Kathleen," said Mam. "And your costume is lovely. Your Aunty Mary worked a miracle with those curtains and that bit of eiderdown. You're a walking haberdashery department, and no one would ever guess!"

Polly came in with a grin. "You're a lot better, all of a sudden," she said to Mam.

"I am," said Mam. "I've turned a corner, Mary. I feel as if I could do heaps and kill dead things."

"Well, don't try that, now," said Polly.

"No," said Mam. "I'll take it easy. But there's one little job I have to do for this daughter of mine."

"What's that, Mammy?" I asked.

"Bring me my workbasket," she said.

Mystified, I went back into the kitchen and took the large wicker workbasket from under the dresser, where she always kept it.

"While we were waiting for the blue material to become a remnant," Mam said, opening up the basket, "I was starting to gather some colored embroidery threads. And I have some nice little Celtic knot patterns that I traced out of a library book. What do you think of that?"

She pulled out a fistful of colors, like a rainbow, purple and yellow and red and white, and spread them all out on the bedspread. Then she reached back into the workbasket and brought out a piece of greaseproof paper, on which were penciled two simple but beautiful designs of interlocking loops.

"Now," said Mam. "My eyes are tired, and I can't thread the needles, but if you and Mary will do that, I'll have no trouble with the embroidery. Sure, I can do it in my sleep. I'll need a few pins, Kathleen, and a little bit of French chalk, and get out of that dress, child, if you don't want to be embroidered into it. Look sharp, now."

"As the fork said to the knife," said Da automatically. He had just appeared in the doorway. "Alice, asthore, you are surely not going to sit up all night embroidering this child's dress, and you only back from death's door."

"No, Tommy, I'm not. It's going to take me an hour at the most. It will tire me, but it won't kill me. Sure, why did God spare me, if it wasn't to be of help to my children? Go down to the pump in the yard, like a good man, and haul us up some water, and then you can put on the kettle to keep us going. Make yourself useful."

It took more than an hour, even with Polly and me doing the threading and handing Mam the colors as she needed them, and Da pouring the tea "to keep us going," as Mam said.

She looked drained by the time she'd finished, but the green dress was transformed from something quite nice but rather ordinary into what it was supposed to be—an Irish dancing costume. The Celtic knot on the bodice glowed with color and brought the dull green of the fabric alive. It was a costume fit for a dancing champion, topped off with Polly's green beret. We stuck the feather from Mam's best hat on the side.

"She'll dance a merry dance in that," said Da.

I would; I knew I would.

"She'll do her best," said Mam, "as she always does."

I glowed with pleasure. Maybe God wasn't cross with me after all. Mother Rosario always said our prayers are often answered in unexpected ways. There was no doubt about it, you couldn't be up to God. You never knew what He was going to do next. That must be what Mother Rosario meant when she said, "God's ways are not our ways."

14 *Curtains*

Angela and Nell were on the very first bench at the front of the Father Mathew Hall. They had strewn coats and scarves and bags all along the bench, keeping places for people. I waved at them when I saw them, and I sent Lily and Madge and Patsy up to join them, so they would be able to see. I was sorry Mam couldn't be there, but Polly had promised to do her level best to come. She had important business to see to first, she'd said, but she'd try to make it. I couldn't imagine anything more important than the *feis*, but grown-ups—even Polly—obviously had other priorities.

Mrs. Maguire was having conniptions behind the stage. She was resplendent in gold and black, and on her heaving shoulder was a huge Tara brooch, like the ones she'd had made for her dancers, only about ten times larger. Her hair, which was usually combed back off her face and worn in a loose ribbon, was all piled up in magnificent curls and wisps. She really did look a bit like Queen Maeve, or maybe Queen Maeve's mother, as Brigid Mullane whispered to me. She was pulling at all her pupils, criticizing their dresses, their *brats*, their hairstyles, their stockings, their dancing poms, even their mothers, in some cases. Nothing was right, in her view.

One or two of the older ones had had "the audacity," as Mrs. Maguire said with a hiss, to put color on their faces—not real rouge, but "Messenger Red," as we called it. They soaked the cover of the *Sacred Heart Messenger*, a holy magazine that most families got, which was a lovely strong red color, till the ink ran, and used the ink to put color on their cheeks and lips. Mrs. Maguire threatened to send them home and never let them darken her door again, brazen, pagan straps that they were, letting down their dancing school, their families, their country even. They might as well have burned the Irish flag or joined the British Legion, as far as Mrs. Maguire was concerned, as put rouge on their cheeks. I was glad I hadn't let Polly talk me into wearing that lipstick of hers, but I bit my lips all the same, to put a bit of color into them.

Girls with short hair had parted it neatly and put green ribbons in it. My hair was done up in ringlets after a night of torture with my scalp all stretched and sore and covered in knotted rags. But now the ringlets were cascading down my shoulders. That was Polly's word for it, "cascading," and I loved the sound of it, though of course I wouldn't say it out loud in case someone thought I was looking for notice.

Tess O'Hara appeared with Annie. They had been allowed to enter at the last moment, mainly because Mrs. Maguire didn't want their mothers making a fuss. Tess was wearing a gorgeous soft sky blue wool costume, with matching *brat* and a pretty little tam-o'-shanter perched on the side of her head. She had her sister Betty with her, who was got up in exactly the same outfit. So that's what had happened to my lovely blue material! The O'Haras had nabbed it and had it made up into matching outfits for Tess and Betty. There's no doubt it was a lovely color, but now that I saw it made up, I could see that it wasn't right for Irish dancing costumes. Polly had been spot on about that. Green was much better, and not so showy, either.

Tess took one look at me and said *mar dhea* to Annie and Betty, but as loudly as she could, so that everyone could hear, "I believe Kathleen Murphy's costume is made out of a pair of curtains! I ask you!" She did a little twirl around as she said it, pretending she was checking to see that her hem was even all the way around but really showing off her soft blue dress.

I just went on brushing my hair quietly and didn't let on I heard what Tess was saying, but if I could have got hold of Patsy and Lily, I would have given them a good quizzing. Madge was old enough to know better, but those little girls would hang you sometimes, the things they would let out. Tess was laughing loudly now, a forced sort of a laugh, like a horse with a cold, and pointing in my direction, and Annie was, too, but I made out I didn't notice a thing, though my cheeks were burning. I swung my hair forward to hide my face and said nothing. I'd learned long ago that the silent treatment was usually the best way to deal with Tess.

She soon got tired of being ignored and went off to torment some other poor creature. Anyway, I had more important things to worry about than where my costume came from.

I was very nervous about the competition. What with Mam being so sick and all the fuss about the costume, I'd missed the last couple of dancing classes before the *feis*, and I hadn't danced, bar skipping up the stairs at home and doing the odd slither around the bedroom floor, for ages. The more I tried to run through the steps in my head, the more terrified I became that I would go completely blank as soon as I stood up.

When my name was called, I felt a rush of fear, my stomach seemed to sink onto the floor of my pelvis, my heart flew upwards and lodged somewhere in my throat, and for a moment, everything went black before my eyes and I wanted to get sick.

"Kathleen Murphy!" Mrs. Maguire hissed and poked me in the back. I stumbled out onto the stage, my legs suddenly feeling as if they were made of putty. I couldn't imagine how they were going to hold me up, much less dance. And still there was no sign of Polly. She was going to miss my dance—if ever I did manage to move my feet.

"Right, Saint Bernadette," I whispered, with my eyes closed. "Don't let me down now. Just get me through this. I don't have to win, I don't even have to dance well. I just have to get through it without falling over."

I opened my eyes then and stared down into the audience, but it was a big, moving, babbling, shifting blur. That was good. I think it would have finished me if I could have made out people I knew. Maybe Polly was out there somewhere, but I was kind of glad that I couldn't see her.

I put my weight on my left foot and stood with my right foot poised, wondering what on earth I was going to do when the music started, because I couldn't remember even the very first step of the dance. But as soon as I heard the squeezebox leading into my tune, everything that had happened over the past few weeks flew out of my head, and the knowledge of the steps came flooding back.

The split second the bar note sounded, I leaped into

action. This was it. Either my legs were going to give way under me and I was going to end up in a heap on the floor with Polly's green curtains all around me, or I was going to dance my heart out. I gave one big, joyful bound and gave myself up to the dance, and the dance did me proud.

I kicked and soared and pranced and whirled, stepped and twirled and spun and flew, tripped and skipped and skimmed and sailed, all over that stage. I hardly knew where I was, and I was completely oblivious to the audience, the strange hall, even the adjudicator, though I knew she must be out there somewhere in the blur of humanity beyond the stage, watching carefully and taking notes. I didn't care about that. I was filled with the joy of the dance, and I didn't give a rattling toss about Tess O'Hara and her sky blue frock and her snooty ways. All I wanted was for the music never to stop, so that I could dance and twinkle and leap in its magic nets forever.

The music did stop, of course, and I did, too; and as soon as I stopped, I knew it was just as well that the music had, because suddenly I was worn out, weak-kneed and panting, fit to collapse.

A terrific noise started up out of nowhere. I thought maybe the roof was coming down or a tremendous thunderstorm had started up, and I stood there, as if nailed to the stage, waiting to be overwhelmed by whatever force it was that had set this thunderous sound in motion. I breathed deeply, blinking and looking around me, still standing center stage, with my toes pointed in front of me and my knee crooked, as I had been taught. Then I realized what the noise was, and I started to smile. It wasn't a natural disaster or a storm. It was applause, a thunderous clapping and stamping of feet and rocking of chairs. And it was for me, for me and my dance. I beamed. I beamed and beamed until my face ached. I felt like the sun, up there on the stage, the center of a little universe, all eyes toward me, and me beaming and radiating triumph and pleasure and gratitude and exhaustion all at once.

I made a little curtsy, and then I tripped quickly and lightly offstage.

"She's so light on her feet," I could hear people say,

as I flew down the steps at the side of the stage. "It's like watching feathers floating on the breeze," some poetic type said. "She's a champion, that's for sure."

They were talking about me, but I'd lost interest now. I wanted to see if Polly was there. I needed to know that she'd seen me dancing. I wanted her to be able to tell my mam about it. Madge and the others wouldn't have the words to describe it, I knew that, and I couldn't describe it myself, but Polly would be able to tell it all with great panache.

I stood near the top of the hall, by the stage, and I scanned the rows and rows of people. A figure was coming toward me, but I couldn't make it out properly in the semi-dusk of the seething room.

"Polly?" I called uncertainly. It couldn't be Polly, though; it was too big and blustering. I was right. It was Mrs. Maguire.

"*Maith thú, a Chaitlín!*" she was saying delightedly, pumping my hand. "Well done, Kathleen! That was a champion performance if ever I saw one. You're my star pupil, do you know that? I'm proud to be your teacher."

I smiled nervously at her. I wasn't used to having

my hand shaken, and I certainly wasn't used to people being proud to be my teacher. I kept on smiling, and at the same time I was trying to look around Mrs. Maguire's bulk to see if I could catch a glimpse of Polly's flying figure and wide smile.

Mrs. Maguire moved away then, after giving my hand one last good yank, to talk to another pupil's mother, and as she did so, I spotted Polly, hanging back, waiting for me to finish my conversation with my teacher.

I was so glad to see her. I waved, and she came running forward and scooped me into a tight, tight hug, whirling me around and around the floor at the side of the rows of seats, till I could hardly breathe.

"Did you see me?" I asked when she finally let me go.

"I only caught the end of it, love," she said, "but you were brilliant, absolutely brilliant. You weren't dancing. You were flying!"

"That's what it feels like," I said. "Flying."

Polly and I found two chairs near the back. We had to sit through all the other competitors in my group. Some of them were good, I thought, but Polly kept whispering, "Not as good as Kathleen Murphy."

"Don't be silly," I said. "You're biased."

When all the dancers were finished, there was a long delay, while the adjudicator scratched her head and wrote things down and whispered to her assistant. At last she stood up on stage and started a big long speech about something called standards and the importance of Irish dancing to the soul of the nation—all Mrs. Maguire sort of stuff that I wasn't a bit interested in. Polly wasn't either. I could see that she was shuffling uneasily on her chair.

At last, though, the adjudicator started to announce the medalists, beginning with third place.

Brigid Mullane.

I clapped like mad. I was delighted for Brigid. She wasn't my favorite person, but I liked her well enough. If she hadn't been in Tess's gang, we might even have been friends.

Then came another girl that we didn't know, from Mrs. Brady's dancing school. She got the next medal. We clapped politely for her, too.

Polly gripped my elbow when the adjudicator

rustled her papers and said, "And now, for the overall winner in this competition. The medal for first place goes to—" she stopped and looked over her glasses. "Ahem," she said. "Sorry, can't find the name here."

I closed my eyes and whispered another prayer to my friend, Saint Bernadette. "Look," I said, "I don't expect to win. I'm glad enough to have got through it. But if I do win, I won't promise to be a nun, because I don't think I'd make a very good nun, and I think God has been trying to let me know that these last few weeks. But I'll light another candle in your grotto on Monday morning and say a decade of the rosary."

"Kathleen Murphy!" said the adjudicator at last, as if surprised to have found my name after all.

The hall erupted. It was like after I'd danced—thunder, crashing and banging, stamping of feet, even a few whistles. Polly pinched my elbow in her excitement and screeched in my ear, "You did it, you did it! I knew you were a champ!"

"Thanks, Saint Bernadette," I whispered. "I owe you one."

"Katsie, Katsie!" I could hear Lily's piping little

voice in the middle of it all. "Katsie won!"

"Go on," Polly said. "Get up there and take the medal off the poor woman and let her go home to her tea. Sure, can't you see she's dying to get out of here? She must be exhausted watching all those baby elephants clumping about the stage!"

I stood up and made my way through the cheering crowd to the front. I gave Nell and Angela and my sisters a big grin as I passed them. Lily was waving the rag doll in the saffron dress at me and practically bursting with pride. I winked at her, and she waved the doll even harder. Madge had to hold on to the waistband of her skirt to keep her from jumping up and following me onto the stage.

"Say something," said the adjudicator to me when I was beside her. "Your public wants to hear from you."

She made a sweeping gesture to the audience, who were still stamping and clapping and whistling.

I wasn't prepared for this. What was I going to say? "Thank you," I tried, but my voice came out really tiny. Then I swallowed and tried again. This time I managed to make myself heard.

"Thank you! Thank you!" The cheering started again. Then I thought of something I wanted to say. "I would just like to tell you all something," I announced.

The noise died down.

"There is a rumor going around," I said, and now my voice was much louder. The hall became quieter still. Everyone was listening. "There is a rumor going around that my costume was made out of a pair of curtains."

A ripple of laughter went around the room, and people rustled in their seats, embarrassed and amused at the same time.

I wasn't embarrassed anymore, though—just very glad to have a costume at all.

"Well," I said, "I want to tell you . . . that it's true."

More laughter, and a few whistles.

"Thank you, Polly. Thank you, Mam."

Then I took my medal and I ran down the steps and out into the afternoon air.

"Well!" said Polly, who had followed me out. "What possessed you to say that? Sure, it's good-bye to any dignity for the Murphy family now!" She was grinning like mad, though. "We'll all go down in history as the people who dress their children in household drapery!"

"Polly," I said, "I wish we were rich."

"So do I, pet, so do I."

"But, well, there's no point in worrying about it, is there? I've decided not to mind about being poor so much. Though I still do wish we were rich."

"You're a bit muxed ip," said Polly.

"No, I'm not, not really. Tess O'Hara thinks she can have one over on me by passing remarks about me and my family, but if I just say, 'Yes, that's right, my dress is made out of a pair of curtains. We are poor, but we do our best . . .' then it takes the harm out of it, doesn't it?"

"It does," said Polly, "especially when you win the competition in those very same curtains! Tess O'Hara can put that in her pipe and smoke it, so she can. Come on, let's go and get those little sisters of yours and head off home to tell your mam and da all about it and show them your medal. They'll be delighted for you. And I have a special cake at your house for us all to share."

"A cake from Jacob's?" I asked.

Everyone knew that Jacob's made the best cakes in Dublin. People only had them on very special occasions, though, because they were very dear.

"Wait and see," said Polly.

15 *The Cake from Jacob's*

Mam was up and dressed when we got home. She was sitting in an armchair by the window, looking pale, but with a little smile on her lips. She had a blanket over her knees and a shawl around her shoulders.

Da was reading the paper by the range as usual.

"How did you do?" Mam asked when she saw me.

"Yes, tell us how you did, alannah," said Da, lowering the paper.

"Well," I said, helping Lily off with her coat, "we're very tired. It's a long walk from Church Street to Pimlico. The little ones are whacked."

"But did you dance well, Kathleen?" asked Mam.

"Did I dance well?" I asked Madge and Patsy and Lily, and I gave them all a big wink.

They stood around and stuffed their fists into their

mouths to keep from laughing.

Madge nodded. "Quite well," she said and giggled.

"Not bad," said Patsy.

"She won!" said Lily, and she jumped up and down. She couldn't keep it in any longer. She grabbed Eddy by the hands and danced around with him. "Ring a ring a rosy," she sang, "Kathleen won a medal. Asha, asha, they all fell down!" She was a great one for dancing around the place. Maybe she would be a dancer one day, too.

"She didn't!" said Mam. "Did you, Kathleen?"

"Yes," I said, and I pulled the medal out of my coat pocket to show her. It was lovely. It had a Celtic design on one side, and it gleamed and shone in the light of the afternoon sun.

"You're a great girl," said Mam. "I always knew it. Mother Rosario was right when she said you were talented. We'll have to sew that medal onto a sash for you right away!"

"And there'll soon be more to keep it company, I'm sure," said Da.

Maybe he was right. Maybe this was the first of many

medals I would win, but I didn't think I'd ever feel as proud again as I did today, with my first-ever medal.

"We'll have our tea first, though," said Polly. "And I have a treat." She was grinning away, like a child who had got a special present for Christmas and was dying to show it off.

There was a large cardboard box standing on the table. I couldn't work out how Polly had known I was going to win a medal. Suppose I hadn't won? Would she still have produced her celebration treat?

Polly opened the box and drew out the biggest white cake we'd ever seen. It was covered in smooth white icing and all decorated with perfect little icing rosebuds and silvery balls. It had its own special round silvery tray with horseshoes embossed on it.

We all stared. We'd never seen anything like it. It was beautiful, like some wonderful snow palace, far too gorgeous to eat.

"Eh," said Madge at last, "that looks like a wedding cake!"

"It is," said Polly, with a tiny nervous grin.

"A Jacob's wedding cake!" said Mam. "My goodness!"

"Who's getting married?" Madge asked.

"I am," said Polly. She was all shiny in the face. "I mean, I *did*. This morning, at six o'clock Mass in Adam and Eve's."

"What?!" said Mam.

"What?" said everyone.

"Mary! You never said . . ." said Da.

The whole family erupted in questions, then crowded around Polly, pulling at her clothes, kissing her, hugging her, talking nineteen to the dozen.

I stood back. I felt let down with a clunk, as if someone had said they were going to take away my medal and give it to someone else. What had Polly been thinking of? And what about all our lovely plans? Would we not live in a garret and paint our toenails and have brandy flips for breakfast? Was it all my eye?

I turned away and tucked my medal into a drawer of the dresser. It had lost its shine for me. While I was at it, I pulled out a clean napkin I found in the drawer and gave my eyes a wipe. I knew I should be glad for Polly, but all I could feel was disappointment.

"Kathleen!" Polly called, and I turned around.

She raised her eyebrows at me, waiting for me to say something.

I couldn't say what I felt, but I had to say something. "I . . . hope you'll be very happy, Polly," I said stiffly, "yourself and Bill."

Polly stared at me and said nothing. A silence fell on the room.

Then Polly said, "I . . . I didn't marry Bill, Kathleen—and everyone. I married Shamy Macnamara. Sure, you all knew I would in the end, didn't you?"

She tried a little laugh, but nobody laughed with her. We knew no such thing. All we knew was that Shamy Macnamara drove Polly mad.

"But you said—" I began.

"I said a lot, Kathleen, but Shamy is a grand man and . . . the truth of it is, we're going to America! Imagine! I'll be like Scarlett O'Hara in no time, you'll see, all *la-di-dah* with a feather in my cap."

"America!" Mam was shocked. I could hear it in her voice. America was a terrible long way away. "God bless us and save us! When—"

"Next month," Polly went on. There were two little

red spots of excitement high up on her cheeks. She was gabbling at a great rate, as if she couldn't get her story out fast enough. "Shamy has an uncle over there, and he can get Shamy a job. Me, too, if I want one. We have our tickets bought. In the names of Mr. and Mrs. Macnamara. We have a cabin, all to ourselves. Imagine, the style of it!"

"But what possessed you to run away and get married at the crack of dawn, Mary?" asked Mam.

"Why did you keep it a secret?" asked Madge, her eyes wide with amazement.

"*I* can keep a secret," said Lily.

"No, you can't," said Patsy. "You'd burst!"

"I'd have waited till you were well, Alice," said Polly, twisting a hankie in her fingers, "and given yous all a day out, but Lent is starting next week, and then we couldn't be married for a whole six weeks, and the ship would have sailed without us. Six o'clock this morning was the only time the priest could fit us in. You wouldn't believe the number of people who want to get married in the week before Lent!"

"But you never said a thing!" said Mam, still shocked.

"Well, this was Kathleen's day," said Polly. "I knew how much she'd been looking forward to it. I couldn't just suddenly announce that I was getting married that very morning. It would have taken the wind out of her sails entirely."

I dabbed at my eyes quickly and tried not to sniffle. I didn't want to cry on Polly's wedding day, but she *had* taken the wind out of my sails all right, even if she'd tried not to.

"Well!" said Mam. "You're a dark horse."

"But what about Bill?" I asked, when I could trust myself to talk. "The one with the smoldering eyes, the fellow who looks like Rhett Butler, what about him?"

"He . . . he's no good, Kathleen," Polly said quietly. "He's a right bowsie."

"What do you mean? I thought he was gorgeous."

"He is," said Polly with a sad little smile. "But he's a bowsie all the same. Not a patch on Rhett Butler. I found out he'd been two-timing me, Kathleen. So that was that."

"But why did you need to go and get *married?*" I practically shouted at her. "What about being an old maid in a garret with me? What about eating chocolates in bed and going to Bewley's for afternoon tea?"

"Ah, Kathleen," said Polly, her eyes clouding over, "I wish . . ." But she didn't say what she wished.

Then she started suddenly fussing around, back to her old jolly self, giving orders, flying about.

"Get out the best china, Madge, it's a celebration. A double celebration. Shamy will be here any minute to help me cut the cake. Have we a bread knife? Patsy, you get it, will you? Lily, you can put out the cups, but don't break them, now—carry them one at a time. Tommy Murphy, make yourself useful and wet the tea!"

"We haven't got any best china," said Madge, "only one plate that belonged to Granny Murphy, with roses on it and goldy paint around the rim."

"That's it, then, that's the best china. Bring it here, and mind you don't drop it or I'll drop your head!"

Polly was back to her normal self, all laughs and nonsense, but I noticed she didn't ask me to join in the tea preparations. *She's a great one for proverbs, but what about "Marry in haste, repent at leisure"?* I thought bitterly to myself.

"Why?" I mouthed at her, when I caught her eye.

She pulled me into a corner and spoke softly. "Because that's what people *do*, Kathleen, grown-up people. They make a life together. I don't want to spend the rest of my days making biscuits, and forever poor. You know it's no fun being poor—you said as much yourself this very day. This is a new start for me."

"But Shamy Macnamara!" I hissed.

"Shamy's a good man," Polly said firmly, "and he loves me, Kathleen."

I wasn't a bit happy about any of it, but I hugged Polly all the same, and I tried to forgive her about the garret. And maybe she was right. You couldn't live on fantasy and afternoon tea at Bewley's. I could see that.

The top step of the stairs creaked.

"That'll be Shamy!" said Polly, and she flew out to meet him, the two little red spots on her cheeks flaming up again.

Seconds later, she came in again, dragging Shamy by the hand.

"Murphys!" she announced, giving a little flounce. "Meet my husband, Mr. James Aloysius Macnamara!"

"I thought his name was Shamy," said Lily, looking up at the couple.

"It is," said Polly. "That's just his posh name."

"Is he our uncle?" asked Patsy.

Polly went off in a ripple of laughter, as if Patsy had cracked some great joke. "I suppose he must be," she said.

It was a bit funny all right, to be suddenly presented with an uncle you hadn't had the day before.

Shamy looked at the floor the whole time. He was all dressed up in a brown suit and a stiff collar, and he didn't look very comfortable.

"You're very welcome to the family, Shamy," said Mam, and she put out her hand to him.

Shamy got red and looked harder than ever at the floor, even while he was shaking Mam's hand.

"Mrs. Macnamara," said Da, "will you pour the tea or will I?"

"Oh!" said Polly, with a start. "That's me! The cake, the cake! We have to cut the cake! Shamy, come here!"

Shamy turned from Mam, and Polly handed him the bread knife.

"We have to do it together," said Polly. "It's part of the whole thing. Working together, you see, that's what marriage is."

"Yes," said Shamy, the very first word he had uttered since coming into the room, and he gripped the bread knife.

Polly put her hand over his, and together they cut the cake. It made a groaning sound as the knife sliced through it. It was bursting with fruit, we could see as soon as it was cut.

We all shouted "Hip-hip-hurray," and Da picked up a teacup and said in a loud voice, "Ladies!" That was us, me and Mam and the girls. Eddy was too small to count. "Ladies, I give you the bride and groom!"

We all picked up our cups then and we waved them in the air and repeated Da's words, "The bride and groom. The bride and groom. The bride and groom." We chinked our cups and drank a solemn toast and tried to look as pleased as we could, for Polly's sake.

Madge started handing around slices of cake.

Polly pushed her plate aside. "I couldn't," she said. "I've had enough excitement for one day."

She turned to me then, and waved her teacup again and said out loud, "And the Irish dancing champion! The first-place medalist! Miss Kathleen Lightfoot Murphy, the Pimlico Prancer, headed for stardom!"

"Stardom!" said Da with a laugh.

"Don't laugh, Tommy Murphy," said Polly. "That girl will go far, you mark my words. I'm sure I'll be hearing about her all the way over in America."

"'The Pimlico Prancer!'" I said. "Don't dare say those words outside this house, Polly Macnamara, or my life won't be worth living." But I was pleased all the same, and I started to smile.

"It will," said Polly, "you'll see. You're going to have a great life, Kathleen Murphy. You will leave the Tess O'Haras of this world in the ha'penny place, just like you did today. But there's one thing—never again will I make you a dress out of a pair of curtains. That's a once-in-a-lifetime experience!"

"Like getting married," I said.

"Like getting married," said Polly.

"Polly?" I asked. I'd been getting a few answers to my questions lately, and I thought I might try another one.

"If you're a Mrs., now that you're married, but you were a Miss yesterday, and if Shamy is a Mr. and he's married now too, why wasn't he a Master yesterday?"

"Well!" said Polly, and she thought for a minute. Then she said, "Ask me no questions, and I'll tell you no lies."

She was turning into one of them—the grown-ups who wouldn't answer questions! *It must be marriage that did it*, I thought.

Maybe I'd stick with being an old maid in a garret after all, even if Polly wasn't going to keep me company. Yes, that's what I would do. I'd miss Polly dreadfully, but she would surely be home on holidays sometimes, and maybe I could go over to America to visit her when I got older.

I wasn't going to give up on my dreams just because Polly had decided to become Mrs. Shamy Macnamara. My garret would have to be a big one, because I'd need a space for my dancing classes. I was going to be a much better teacher than Mrs. Maguire—I'd teach girls how to fly—and I would charge a shilling a lesson. I wasn't going to settle for being poor any more than Polly was.

I would paint my toenails any color I liked and I wasn't going to bother my head going to Bewley's for tea—I would send out to Bewley's for sticky buns any time I felt like it, and they would send everything around on a tin tray with a Japanese lady on it, and I would give the messenger boy threepence for his trouble. And that famous garret of mine was going to be stuffed full of gleaming Irish dancing medals that I'd won at *feiseanna* all over the country until it was sparkling like a treasure cave. I was going to be a medal millionaire!

Then and Now ♦ *A Girl's Life*

IRELAND

Irish men, women, and child[ren] danced outdoors at the crossroad[s] in the 1800s.

Kathleen's Irish dancing lessons were part of an Irish movement called the Celtic Revival, which started in the 1890s. This revival was Ireland's way of reclaiming and celebrating its traditional culture and history after centuries of occupation and rule by Britain. In dancing schools from Dublin to Cork, Irish girls like Kathleen learned to dance the jigs, reels, and hornpipes that were an important part of Ireland's heritage.

A little more than a decade before Kathleen's story takes place, Ireland signed a treaty of independence from Britain. Even so, the Irish people were divided over the terms of this treaty—so divided, in fact, that the island of Ireland split into two states. Northern Ireland maintained the link with Britain whereas the

Irish Free State, or *Eire*, in the southern part of Ireland, severed all political ties to Britain. Catholics were in the majority in the Irish Free State, while Northern Ireland had a Protestant majority. Some Catholics left Northern Ireland rather than live under Protestant rule.

Even though Northern Ireland chose to remain part of the United Kingdom, many people in the Irish Free State still wanted Ireland to be one country. In 1922, a bitter civil war broke out in the Irish Free State over the treaty that divided Ireland. The civil war was relatively short, but families and friends remained deeply divided for years. Unionists like Kathleen's mother supported the treaty and wanted to rebuild an alliance with England, whereas nationalists like Kathleen's father wanted total independence from Britain and a united Ireland.

Some of the Catholics who fled Northern Ireland arrived in Eire with only what they could carry.

Dev, shown here leading a protest in the 1920s, eventually served Ireland as both prime minister and president.

In 1937, when Kathleen's story takes place, the outspoken nationalist Eamon de Valera, or "Dev," drafted the Irish Free State's first constitution. Like other Irish leaders, Dev believed that encouraging traditional Irish dance, music, and design as well as the use of the Irish language, or *Gaelic*, reinforced Irish identity and was good for the country. Eventually, the Irish Free State became the *Republic of Ireland*—usually referred to as *Ireland*.

The worldwide depression of the 1930s affected Ireland, but because of the earlier decades of political strife, economic turmoil, and high unemployment, many Irish were already poor. The Depression just made them poorer than they had been before. In cities like Dublin and Cork, jobs

An Irish dancing champion from the 1930s in a dancing costume decorated with Celtic designs.

Many poor families like Kathleen's lived in formerly grand Dublin tenement houses like these.

were scarce, and working-class families like Kathleen's struggled to make ends meet.

Dublin, Ireland's capital, was a city of neighborhoods. Kathleen's family lived in a crowded and densely populated neighborhood known as "The Liberties." Large families often shared only two or three rooms in a house or apartment building, and they were lucky if they had a range to cook on instead of just a fireplace. Indoor plumbing was rare. These crowded conditions were difficult, but relatives and neighbors shared what they had and relied on one another for help and support. The church also played a large part in people's lives, and most children attended Catholic school.

Families enjoyed attending *feiseanna*, which were music, dance, and drama competitions. As Irish dancing grew in popularity, costumes embellished with traditional Irish designs became more popular, too, and sometimes medals were awarded for costume design.

Even a plain wool dress like Kathleen's became a dancing costume when it had a cape-like *brat* attached at the shoulders and was embellished with Celtic embroidery.

Today, Irish people live all over the world. Many had to leave Ireland during the mid-1800s because of famine, but their descendants have kept ties to Ireland through Irish music and dance. People of all nationalities enjoy Irish celebrations and performances, and Irish dancing has grown in popularity in recent years worldwide, thanks to television and lavish stage productions such as *Riverdance*.

The Republic of Ireland today is a vital and vibrant country that celebrates its Celtic heritage. It has a strong economy

Modern Irish dance costumes are elaborate and brightly colored.

Lively performances sparked renewed interest in Irish dancing.

based on agriculture, tourism, and hi-tech industry. The island of Ireland is still divided into two states, and the ongoing and sometimes violent conflict between nationalists and unionists continues to challenge the Irish people. But in recent years, the Irish and British governments have worked together with Northern Ireland, and the level of violence has dropped.

Today, girls in Ireland stay in school at least until age 16, and many go on to university before pursuing careers. Some women go into politics; in fact, Ireland has had two women presidents, both of whom have worked hard to improve life for everyone in Ireland.

Most Irish schools today require students to wear uniforms.

Glossary

Words in italic are Irish (Gaelic), and the pronunciations are only approximate. Other words are either anglicizations of Irish words or are ordinary English words, in many cases used with a special meaning in Ireland or specifically in Dublin.

a chailíní *(ah KOLL-een-ee)*—girls (to address a group of girls; otherwise, *cailíní*, the plural of *cailín*, or girl)

a Chaitlín *(ah KATH-ee)*—Kathleen, in Gaelic, when chaitlín is addressed directly

adjudicator—a judge

alannah *(ah-LAHN-nah)*—my child (term of endearment, from Gaelic *leanbh*, meaning "child")

aon, dó, trí, ceathair, cúig, sé, seacht *(ayn, dtho, three, kah-HAHR, koo-ig, shay, shakth)*—the Gaelic numbers one through seven

asthore *(ah-STHOHR)*—my darling, my love (from Gaelic *stór*, meaning "treasure")

biscuits—cookies

bold—naughty

bowsie—bad fellow, cad (a word specific to Dublin)

brandy flip—eggnog flavored with brandy and sugar

brat *(pronounced, roughly, "broth," though the Irish T sound is partway between the English T and TH sounds)*—a flag or a large flat piece of fabric worn as a shawl or cape; in Irish dancing, a short, simple shawl, with a decorative or symbolic function only, that is attached to the shoulders of a dress

brosna *(BRUSS-nah)*—kindling to make a fire

Ceist ag éinne? *(Keshth ehg aynyah)*—Any questions?

Celtic *(KEL-tik)*—referring to the language and culture of the early people of Ireland

chun glóire Dé agus onóra na hÉireann *(hun gloh-ihr jay ogg-uhs ohn-oh-yah heh-rihn)*—"to the glory of God and the honor of Ireland"

colcannon *(KOLL-kahn-on)*—potatoes and cabbage mashed with milk and butter

colleen—girl

copy—a school exercise book (short for "copybook")

crawthumping—behaving in an excessively pious manner

Dev—Eamon de Valera, who was a government leader at the time of this story

fag—cigarette

feis *(fesh)*—competitive festival, with competitions in all the performance arts: dancing, singing, playing musical instruments, drama, and verse-speaking

feiseanna *(FESH-ehn-nah)*—plural of feis

fizz bag—a paper bag of sherbet powder, usually accompanied by a jelly lollipop as a scoop or a licorice tube through which to suck the powder

fringe—hair bangs

gom—idiot

(in the) ha'penny place—far behind, in a position of no importance

Jubilee nurse—public health nurse

let on—pretend (for example: "*Let on you have a limp*" means "Pretend you have a limp"; "*Don't let on you see him*" means "Pretend you don't see him.")

lino—linoleum

maith thú *(MAH-hoo)*—"Well done!"

mar dhea *(MAHR-yah)*—untranslatable, but corresponds roughly to a nod and a wink; an expression used to show that the rest of the sentence is not to be believed

moidhered *(MOY-derd)*—bothered, irritated, intensely annoyed

my eye—nonsense, pretense

nappy—diaper (short for *napkin*)

ninepence—three-quarters of a shilling

poms—close-fitting, lightweight leather dancing slippers, a mispronunciation of "pumps"

porridge—cooked oatmeal

press—cupboard

rawmaysh *(raw-MAYSH)*—nonsense (noun), talk nonsense (verb) (from Gaelic *raiméis*)

rip—a mean or spiteful woman

rise—to take a rise out of or get a rise out of a person is to annoy or tease them

shilling—one-twentieth of a pound, or twelve pennies; one-and-six(pence) means one and a half shillings, one-and-nine(pence) means one and three-quarter shillings, and so on

(holy) show—a terrible mess, disgrace, embarrassment

shower—crowd or group of people, always used negatively or disapprovingly (for example, "I wouldn't trust that shower.")

slat *(pronounced, roughly, "sloth," though the Irish letter T is partway between the English T and TH sounds)*—literally, "yardstick," but particularly a stick used as an instrument of punishment, especially in school

sos *(suss)*—breaktime in school, recess

spaugs *(spogs)*—feet, especially big, awkward feet

strap—badly behaved, sullen girl

swish—very classy and sophisticated

take off—imitate (by way of making fun)

tenement—in Dublin, a large eighteenth-century house once owned by a wealthy family but now run-down and divided into numerous small apartments occupied by poor families, often with parents and several children sleeping together in one room, where they also had to wash, cook, and eat

tuppence—two pence, or two pennies

wireless—radio

wreck of the *Hesperus*—the *Hesperus (HEHS-pehr-uhs)* was a ship that sank and was the subject of a poem by Longfellow; the title of the poem came to be used as a phrase to mean *a mess*, particularly with regard to a person's clothes and personal appearance

Author's Note

The characters in this story are poor people, living in Dublin at a time when Ireland was just emerging as an independent country. Like any new state, Ireland at the time was deeply interested in itself. The people were concerned with what it meant to be Irish, and they spent a lot of energy trying to work that out and find ways of expressing it in their everyday lives. That's really what this story is about.

My parents grew up at around the same time as Kathleen, and lots of the details in this book come from incidents they told me about their childhood, or things I noticed them do and say. Kathleen could almost have been at school with my mother or might have brushed past my grandmother on the bus—and I'm pretty sure I saw Polly crossing the street only last week!

By the time I was growing up, in the 1960s, Ireland had changed. Most people were better off, and we had things like cars and refrigerators. We'd even got our own Irish television channel. But on the inside, people had hardly changed at all. They still spoke and joked and thought and prayed in very much the same way that Kathleen and her family do in this story.

Kathleen could easily still be alive today, but if she'd gone off somewhere at the age of twelve and then came back to Dublin right now, she'd hardly recognize the place: it's choked with traffic, everyone is dressed in jeans, Eastern European and African languages are spoken on the streets, it's noisy and busy and fast—it's a long way from the leisurely paced, easy-going, overgrown village that it was in Kathleen's youth. The Liberties, where Kathleen grew up, still has pockets of poverty, privation, and neglect, but it is abuzz, too, with shops and street markets, students and newcomers, mosques and Asian food stores. It was a joy to wander its streets as I wrote this book, trying to imagine what it was like in 1937. Frawley's is still there, with all its bargains, and so is the church tower clock that struck nine so fatefully for Kathleen on the morning when the story opens . . .